BUTTERFLY TRADECRAFT©

BOOK Six

of the

SECRET BUTTERFLY SERIES™

A NOVEL BY

Rosemary Lightfoot Ness-Bitner

A caution and disclaimer

All characters, events, and conversations in this book are fictional, the product of the author's imagination, or used fictitiously. Any resemblance to actual characters, living or dead, events past or present, localities, or conversations, is entirely coincidental.

If you are offended or stressed by characters' offensive behaviors and expressions of strong opinions about controversial subjects, you are advised and cautioned to not purchase this book or listen to this audio book. If you are a child under the age of eighteen, do not purchase this book or listen to this audio book as it contains erotic adult content. Sexual activity may cause diseases.

THIS BOOK CONTAINS SADISM, MURDER, AND EXPLICIT EROTIC ROMANCE CONTENT. IT IS INTENDED FOR MATURE READERS AND AUDIENCES OVER THE AGE OF EIGHTEEN ONLY. IT MAY BE OFFENSIVE OR STRESSFUL TO SOME READERS. OPINIONS, VIEWS, AND ADVICE GIVEN IN THIS BOOK BY ITS CHARACTERS TO OTHER CHARACTERS, AND BEHAVIORS EXHIBITED AND ADVOCATED BY ITS CHARACTERS DO NOT REFLECT THE OPINIONS, VIEWS, OR ADVICE, OR ADVOCATION OF BEHAVIORS OF, OR BY, THE AUTHOR OR PUBLISHER, OR OF, OR BY, ANY ORGANIZATION OR ENTITY TO WHICH THE AUTHOR OR PUBLISHER ARE AFFILIATED. NEITHER THE AUTHOR, THE PUBLISHER, NOR ANY OTHER PERSONS ASSOCIATED WITH THIS BOOK SHALL BE HELD RESPONSIBLE FOR ANY CONSEQUENCES ARISING FROM THE OPINIONS, VIEWS, ADVICES, BEHAVIORS, OR INTERPRETATIONS EXPRESSED BY THE CHARACTERS IN THIS BOOK; OR, IN ANY OTHER WAY, EXPRESSED IN THIS BOOK, OR BY ITS COVER.

This book is dedicated to lovers and their dreams.

The eBook and print version layouts of BUTTERFLY TRADE-CRAFT were done by Andrea Reider. The cover was created by Cheeky Covers. I am Melanie Monarch, your audio book narrator.

Hello, dear readers and listeners. In BUTTERFLY TRADECRAFT, our sixth book of THE SECRET BUTTERFLY SERIES, Bertie dedicates her considerable management and coaching talents to Marty's burgeoning porn career. With Bertie's help, Marty creates the most riveting, profoundly content rich, and most explicitly salacious erotic films ever produced. Marty's star as the queen of Intimate Artistry now shines more brightly than all other adult film actresses in the wildly popular new genre. Gwendolyn, a wealthy benefactor of Marty's reveals to Marty a fascinating side of herself that no one except Bertie understands.

SECRET BUTTERFLY SERIES ™ CHARACTERS INTRODUCED IN "BUTTERFLY TRADECRAFT©" (MAJOR CHARACTERS ARE BOLDFACED)

Readers reference guide to where a character is introduced.

(CHARACTER, DESCRIPTION OF CHARACTER, AND CHAPTER WHERE CHARACTER IS MENTIONED)

GWENDOLYN, MARTY'S BENEFACTOR, CONFIDANT AND LOVER, (BT), CH7

U, THE UNIVERSAL SPIRIT OF ALL LIVING THINGS, MARTY'S PROTECTOR, BT, CH11

CHAPTER ONE

Fair seed-time had my soul and I grew up fostered alike by beauty and by fear. (William Wordsworth: The prelude)

FRIGHTENED DREAMS

"Tell me Marty, have you ever feared your fans or been afraid something might hurt you?" Bertie continued questioning Marty, trying to gain a full understanding of the young porn star. From her years of coaching and her work with her daughter, Amanda, Bertie knew the best way to gain confidence and trust was to have her charge divulge all the emotions that affected her performances.

"My fans? No, they all love me. I'm not afraid of them. But some times I wake up weirded out or terrified because of my dreams."

"Oh, dreams can be very important. Tell Bertie about them, sweetheart."

"Well, okay. Sometimes I dream I left Mrs. O'Dell's, my shrink, and I needed to catch a bus to get home. But while I'm waiting for the bus a huge sphere comes instead. It opens and there are people inside. I go in and sit down. It takes us to the station, but it's not a bus station. It's the sphere's launch station. Then I notice all the people in the sphere with me are whores, like me.

"Where's our bus?" I asked the woman seated next to me.

"There's no bus today." She speaks. "We're not allowed to go home today. Our sphere is going to the launch pad."

"Suddenly, blinking red lights appear above our heads."

"Why the lights?" I ask another woman. She explains that they will blink like that until, one by one, they turn to green. When they are all green that means that our sphere is cleared to depart, that no other sphere will intersect our path of travel and crash into us.

"Where are we going," I ask.

"To a planet in another star system on the other side of the galaxy. We have to fuck a few hundred astronauts. They've been working there for years."

"Will I ever get back to Earth and see Bob again? I need to be with Bob. I love him."

"Yes, the entire round trip only takes a week."

"I feel pretty okay then because I often leave Bob for a week or two to go to some far away place with a Premium Member, so Bob doesn't need to know I'm fucking astronauts on other planets. He won't worry about me. That's an okay dream, and I usually wake up from that one feeling good, but it is a little weird. I've talked with Mrs. O'Dell about that dream:

"It's a very healthy dream, my dear," she said, "It's your limbic mind preparing your conscious mind to accept my New Modern Morality Standard. Women must become more promiscuous and be willing to go to other worlds and happily fornicate to keep humanity moving forward into outer space; and human space travel will be more harmonious if women and men will accept having multiple sex partners. They'll be more successful when they honor their limbic urges to fornicate.

"This particular dream is an indicator that your mind is rapidly adjusting to limbic thought dominance and the new morality that humans need to move into space. It's progressive for our human species. Your intuitive mind is assuring you that your promiscuity is extremely positive. You are having a healthy evolutionary

progression, dear. You need to seek more opportunities to accelerate your progress towards total immorality. You must share your sexuality with more and more partners."

"Bob also has strange dreams, Bertie. He tells me about them, and then I have weird dreams about his dreams. He sometimes dreams that he's an insect, like he's some kind of beetle; and he's eating this special food that tastes really good. He imagines this food's taste in his dream and says it tastes exactly like my vagina, which he says tastes more delicious than anything in the world.

"Then he realizes that there are other insects and some worms eating this special food too. There are roaches, lice, silverfish, crickets, and ants. Well. Bob feels he needs to keep these other insects away from his food, so he chases them away; and then he wakes up and he desperately wants to have cunnilingus with me. He kisses my vagina for a whole hour after he has that dream; and he tells me he doesn't ever want to lose me.

"Well, his dream gives me nightmares sometimes. I imagine I'm trapped in some tiny room and all these insects are crawling all over me. They are going into my ears, my mouth, my nose, and my eyes; and all of them are going into my brain and eating my brain. It's a horrible dream. After I first heard it, I told Bob to never repeat it to me; but he had it a second time and told me about it. Neither of us knows what his dream means; but now insects frighten me. I don't like seeing them.

"But then there's this other dream Bob has and tells me about:

"He dreams he's this big fat body that crawls along, over the ground. It eats everything and keeps getting fatter. Then, he feels some weird sensation tells him to lie down, curl up and go to sleep. When he awakens, he has wings and he can flutter in the air. And then he panics. He knows he absolutely must find me. He flies for endless days looking for me because he absolutely positively needs to kiss my vagina and put his penis inside me."

"If Bob can't find me, he knows he'll die. He'd feel terrible and unhappy. So, he searches everywhere for me until he finally has me in his arms. Sometimes his dream causes me to have this dream that Bob is coming for me through the sky and we are going to make fabulous love together. When I wake up from that dream, we always make love before we do anything else that day. I love that dream.

"Then there's this other, really bad, dream. I hate it but I keep having it. It always starts out the same. I dream I drive to this place on the other side of town to meet a man in his motel room. I am a prostitute. I have my directions to go to room 73; and I have the name of the man I am supposed to see from my call service. Well, when I get to the motel, I go to room 73, but its door is cemented shut. The housekeeping maid tells me I need to go upstairs, to the other room 73, on the second floor. So, I climbed the stairs to go to that room, but on my way up the stairs I passed a mailman lying dead on the stairs. He has a knife stuck in his back.

"I get to room 73 on the second floor. I put my hand on the door handle and I knock on the door. A man yells out and tells me to go away; that another girl got there before me; and he's right in the middle of getting a blow job. He says:

"You're interrupting us. You need to mind your own business." But I hear some crying and groaning from inside; so, I look through that little glass eye hole in the door. That's when I see that this room is filled with dead and dying people. I ask them through the door what is wrong with them; and they say they are being starved to death because there is no food for them.

"I see their eyes, Bertie. There was no spark of life in them."

"Can I help you?" I ask.

"Yes, go away!" they say. "Our souls are about to leave our bodies. You can't come with us. You must leave us."

"Why can't I come with you?" I ask.

"Because, they're going to bomb again. You must leave."

"*Who's going to bomb?*"

"*The United States Air Force, silly. Stop being stupid.*"

"*What about you?*" I ask. "*Shouldn't you leave, too?*"

"*Don't be so stupid!*" they say. "*Look around you. The whole motel was bombed away except room 73.*"

"*Why is room 73 still here? Doesn't the Air Force know how to bomb?*"

"*Stop asking silly questions. Run!*"

"*But, how can I get downstairs? The rest of the motel got bombed away.*"

"*The stairs are still there.*"

"I looked down at the door handle. Next to it I see the number 2 in bold red lettering. I didn't have any instructions about a second room 73, and I wondered if the number 2 was some kind of a mistake. I called to the man inside about the number 2."

"*Is this number 2 some kind of mistake?*" I ask. "*There's not a 1 on room 73 on the first floor. Does the 2 mean I'm on the second floor?*"

"*It's not a mistake,*" he answers. "*It means it's going to happen again!*"

"*What's going to happen again?*" I ask. I look down at my hands and there is blood on them. That frightens me.

"*You'll see,*" he said.

"*Who did this?*" I ask about the people in the room.

"*He did.*"

"*Who's He?*" I ask.

"*Ask him, he knows,*" he answers.

"*Ask who?*" I yelled.

"*You know,*" he insists.

"*No, I don't know,*" I said, "*Who?*"

"*Him. I told you. Mind your own business. Go home. Leave us alone.*"

I couldn't understand what the man was trying to tell me, so I left.

As I walked back down the stairs the dead mailman lifted his arm and handed me a note. It read: 'Your tights have a hole in them. Everyone can see your butterfly. Stop buying cheap stuff from multi-level marketers. You'll catch a disease.'

I say to the dead mailman: *"I thought you were dead?"*

"I am dead," he says; *"Think of yourself. Get new tights and cover your vagina so you don't catch a disease."*

"My partners don't have diseases," I said, *"There are no diseases to catch."*

"But people can see your vagina," he says.

"I know," I say. *"Don't worry about it. It's not your problem."*

"Can I fuck you?" he asks.

"I don't fuck dead guys," I tell him.

"Why not? What's the big deal? So, I made a stupid mistake. Now I'm dead. I paid for it, okay? Everyone deserves a second chance, don't they"?

"Yes, everyone does, but you're dead. You can't fuck."

"Oh yes, I can. Don't you know anything? The body has no control over my soul, or my cock. Unzip my pants and see what a huge cock I have. You'll love fucking me."

"Why would I love fucking a dead man?"

"Because you have the devil inside you."

"How do you know that?"

"Because you went to room 666, where you keep your victims."

"I went to room 73."

"No, it was 666. You went to 273. That's code for 666. Two times three is six; three times two is six; that's two sixes. Seven times one of the sixes is forty-two; and four and two makes the third six. You can't fool me."

"Why the three sixes?"

"They stand for wanton, crafty, and wicked, six letters in each word, you see. Those words are you. You are wanton, crafty, and wicked. You are the world's number one whore. You are the whore every man wants to fuck."

"But why?"

"Because your courage, cunning and confidence always triumphs over fear, ignorance, and superstition. You crush the nicely nice girls; you've got red blooded lust; That's why. You have an immoral soul. I'd crawl through barbed wire and broken glass to fuck you. I'd die a hundred times to kiss your vagina. Can I fuck you now?"

"Well, I did as the dead man said. I unzipped his pants to see his cock. But he didn't have a cock. Instead, there was this huge, green, and yellow caterpillar inside his pants. I thought it was beautiful. When it saw me, it stopped eating its milkweed leaf. It turned to me and gave me a huge hug with all hundred of its arms. It touched me everywhere; and I loved it. His touches felt wonderful.

"I can't make love with you now," said the caterpillar. *"I'm still eating so I can become big and strong for you. You like big strong cocks, don't you?"*

"Yes, of course I do," I said. *"When will you be big and strong?"*

"Soon, my cock will be wonderful for you. You'll see. You'll want to fuck me all day long. But we must wait until we become butterflies. Then I will flutter with you above the Mexican jungle. We'll make love like crazy; and I'll make you pregnant."

"Then what?" I asked.

"Then you'll lay your eggs. Our spirits will be inside each egg. When we hatch in the warm sun, our spirits will go into humans. I'll come to you then. My spirit will find yours, living inside your human body. I'll find you and join with you and we'll make love every day and every night, forever."

"Well, why can't we make love right now?" I asked.

"Why don't we?" he asks. *"Because I'm dead. Don't you know you're going to die, too?"*

"Why do you say that?" I ask.

"Because," he says. *"They are going to bomb again. Can't you remember anything you are told? You need to find your car and go home. Come and see me later. We'll make love then."*

"Okay," I said. *"I'll be back. Don't go anywhere."*

"Don't be silly. I can't go anywhere. I'm dead."

"Oh, that's right. Well, I've got to go now." Then I left the motel; but, when I got to the parking lot where I left my car, my car was gone. I wasn't sure I left it where I thought I'd left it, so I went walking around the neighboring streets looking for my car. A man in a uniform appeared. He told me my car was in a high-rise garage.

"I didn't park it in a high-rise garage, someone must have moved my car." I spoke.

"It doesn't matter what you thought you did, and I don't give a damn about your opinions." he says. *"All that matters is they are going to bomb again. You need to get your car."*

"But, if they bombed before, how come the high-rise garage is still standing?" I ask. I'm getting impatient with these people.

"Don't ask stupid questions. I'm not here so you can ask me stupid questions, am I clear about that?"

"Yes, you're clear about that."

"Am I clear? I'm asking you if I'm clear!"

"I said you were clear, okay?"

"Good. Now look, do you see that hole in the ground? That's where your car was. They bombed it. Am I clear? I need to be sure that I am clear!" He was angry with me because I questioned him.

"Then how come they didn't hit my car," I asked the obvious question.

"*What are you, some kind of stupid person? I cannot stand stu-pid people! Tell them to stop sending me stupid people! Your car is in the garage, stupid. I'm an important man. Am I clear? I don't have time for any more of your stupid questions. Get your fucking car!*"

"*Will you please help me find my car?*"

"*No, of course not. I told you, I'm an important person and I'm very busy.*" He shook his head emphatically.

"*Why won't you help me?*" I shook my head in dismay.

"*Because the world is out of toilet paper! That's a big deal! Am I clear? What's wrong with you? Don't you know anything?*"

"*Why are you wearing that uniform?*"

"*Because I work for the post office! Don't you know anything? What planet do you live on? Who's your daddy? Get real! Now, at the end of the day, the bottom line is I have to go. I'm very hugely busy. I'm much, much, much too busy to answer any more of your stupid questions!*"

"He shook his head again and pointed to the garage. Then he threw up his hands and walked away from me, cursing about how stupid I was. I went to the garage looking for my car. At the garage, I was climbing stairs and looking on each floor for my car, but every floor was empty. There were no cars in the garage. The man appeared a second time. He told me my car was in the garage basement. So, I walked down endless flights of stairs in my spiked heels. My feet hurt. I got to the basement, but my car was gone.

"I thought I was in the wrong garage, or the uniformed man was mistaken. I decided to leave the garage. As I climbed up the stairs to get to the ground floor and leave the garage, the stairs stopped at this opaque ceiling. I became frightened and I pan-icked. There was this thick plastic ceiling over my head. I pushed hard against it. It was too heavy to lift. I started crying. I thought I was going to die. I went back down a few stairs until I came to a small door. This was odd because the door was not there the first time that I went down the stairs.

"I went through the door and found myself out on the sidewalk; but there was a low chain-link fence between me and the street, and for some reason I knew I had to cross the street. But I knew if I tried to step over the fence my dress would catch and tear; so I walked until I came to a low section of fence. I stepped over it. My dress caught and tore anyway. I walked along a very dirty street that had old newspapers and trash from pizza boxes with rats eating left-over pizzas. I was about to cross the street when this old man yelled:

"There's food around the corner!"

"I realized how hungry I was. I ran around the corner. There were thousands of dirty, poorly dressed people in torn clothes, shuffling forward slowly. I asked a woman why we were in line. She told me it was the only place we could get bread; and she looked at me and laughed. She said:

"You're no better than us. You're just a stupid whore."

"I looked down at my dress. It had mud on it and it was badly torn. I was not presentable. I wondered how I could possibly go back to Apartment number 73 and do a blow job trick or give the dead man a fuck while wearing my filthy dress. Then the woman held up a pocket mirror. I looked in her mirror. I saw my face was no longer beautiful. I had an old wrinkled face. That terrified me. Then the woman said:

"You look terrible. You don't even have any make up. Nobody will even pay you for blow jobs, will they?"

"I was frightened and hungry. I asked her where I could go to buy food. She pointed to a big building far down the street. She said they had meat and vegetables there. That sounded good to me, so I walked and walked for the longest time. My feet hurt and I was getting hungrier as I walked. When I finally got to the building a big strong man was standing in front of huge brass doors. He was like a human guard dog. There was a hungry, mangy dog sitting next to him. The man's muscles bulged out of his shirt. He frightened me. I knew he'd hit me if I tried to get past him. I felt powerless. He stopped me and asked me why I was there. I told him I wanted to buy some food because I was hungry. He said:

"Let me see your money."

"So, I pulled a roll of twenties out of my dress pocket. It was all I had from the five blow jobs I did that day. The man laughed. He said:

"That isn't good money anymore. You need gold or silver to buy food in there."

"I asked him where I could change my money for gold and silver; and he pointed to an old woman seated at a card table. He said:

"She changes gold and silver for chits to buy food inside, but she doesn't take your kind of money anymore. It isn't any good. She can't get gold or silver for it. She stopped taking your kind of money yesterday."

"I looked at the old woman. She looked exactly like the old woman's face I saw in the mirror. That frightened me. I thought I was seeing myself. I asked the big man:

"What can I do?"

"He laughed a big roaring laugh and said:

"You can go away and die, DIE, DIE, DIE." He kept saying *"DIE"* and laughing at me like I was a wretched animal. The word "DIE" echoed off the buildings, like it was being shouted at me by a monster, only now the monster was living inside my own mind. It wouldn't stop screaming and telling me that I needed to die.

"I started crying. I didn't want to die. I thought dying was a terrible idea and I didn't want any part of it. I wanted to live forever. I knew if I could get back to Bob, I would live forever, somehow. I thought that Bob and I might make a baby caterpillar and our spirits would live inside it and it would become a butter-fly. I had to run away from my own voice that told me I needed to die. I thought I might have a disease. I was hungry. I felt weak. I wanted to get away. I started looking for my car again. I couldn't wait to find my car so I could drive away from there. I dreamed I was suddenly going very fast, flying down the road; going so fast that I was passing other cars, and without even being in my car.

"I started screaming because I was going so fast; I was afraid I was going to crash my car; except I was driving by myself without the car. Maybe I was in some kind of driverless car, flying along over the highway without having the car around me. I thought maybe the car was there but it somehow became invisible. I screamed some more because I was getting mad at my car. I wanted to see my car but it wouldn't let me see it.

"Then, my cell phone rang. I answered it. It was Bob. Bob was on the phone asking me where I was and asking me what was wrong. I told him I was hungry and terrified that I might have a disease, and my dress was torn, and I had mud all over me, and I had to die, because there was a hideous monster screaming at me, telling me to die; and the monster was trying to catch me so he could chop me up and feed me to his starving dog; and I couldn't find my car. I felt the monster shaking me and telling me I needed to die. I knew he had his hands on me. And that terrified me. So, I screamed again, as loud as I possibly could. He shook me harder and told me it was time to wake up.

"When I awoke, I found myself in Bob's arms. We were lying in bed and he was holding me tightly close to him. My nighty was soaked through with night sweats. I was still wondering how I ended up in bed with Bob instead of with that dead man, and why I hadn't fucked the dead man; and why I wasn't out walking the streets in my torn dress, all hungry and frightened.

"You're safe," Bob said. "We have food. There's no monster. You're not going to die. We have some gold and silver. You'll never go hungry. You don't have a disease. Your partners are clean. You're not going to get a disease. I'll enable you to keep making erotic movies as long as you want. I love you and I want you to do whatever makes you happy. You'll always have a warm bed and a roof over your head. I'll never let anything bad happen to you. And, I'll always love you no matter how old we are."

"His assurances made me feel better. We made fabulous love, the kind of love I call 'needy love' because I know I need Bob more than anyone else in the world. I know he loves me and I can place my trust in his love. After we made love Bob made us a breakfast of toast and scrambled eggs.

"I was grateful to have Bob in my life and to be alive. I had been terrified that I might go hungry and I never want to go hungry. I know I love him more than anyone else in the world. He understands me and accepts me with all my psychological issues. I couldn't live without that deep understanding and acceptance from my man.

"I've had other similar dreams, but they don't have dying people in them or endings where a man is yelling at me to go away and die. That dream is horrible. When bad dreams start, I remind myself that Bob is there for me and that he loves me, and then those dreams often evaporate into sleep without me dreaming I'm hungry. I keep recalling that bad dream. It makes me realize that I'm terrified of dying. I'm not ready to die. I don't want that day to come, but I know it will come. When it comes, I want to go to a place that loves and accepts whores."

"Sweetheart," Bertie comforted, "you don't need to worry about going hungry. In addition to Bob, George and I will not allow anything bad to happen to you. That's a promise."

Bertie understood what she had in Marty. That was Bertie's genius. She knew how to identify the unique talents, weaknesses, and thoughts that set one person apart from all others. She had often marveled at Amanda's strong legs and how her child loved to jump. Amanda could skip rope for hours; never tiring, long after other girls stopped. Bertie's daughter was perfect clay whom Bertie had molded into Olympic gold.

Bertie no longer had Amanda. But she now had uniquely promiscuous and unapologetically shameless Marty. Marty's limbic zone and vulva were hyper sensitized to seek and express wanton sexuality. The pairing of Marty's limbic desires with her erotically sensitized vulva was the gorgeous young woman's entire reason for living! Uninhibited sexuality; obsessively driven by incurable nymphomania and the mental pain of childhood abandonment made the young nymph Bertie's perfect clay. The nymph's immoral promiscuity was encouraged by her psychologist and enabled by Bob, her live-in lover. Her promiscuous instincts were ideally refined; yet never professionally molded; still raw clay!

Marty's psychological condition did not concern Bertie. Marty's mother opened promiscuity's door when she abandoned her child. Bertie had nothing to do with the events that put Marty on the path of prostitution, or the experiences that caused her psychological fears. Besides, Marty's shrink opined that the cure for her nymphomania was more seductions and much more sex!

Bertie recognized Marty as her fabulous, unique opportunity. She could mold the gorgeous, sex- addicted young woman into performing greatness. She could create the most highly desired erotic film star, ever. As Marty's coach, Bertie understood that she, too, would achieve fame and honors. The deepest reaches of her soul stirred with renewed purpose. She had someone to nurture again! She harbored a profound attraction to the younger woman, both in a loving motherly sort of way; and in an intimate, carnal way. Marty was the best of Bertie's worlds.

CHAPTER TWO

If thou canst death defy, if thy faith is entire, press onward for their eye shall see their heart's desire. (Robert Bridges: Oh, youth whose hope is high)

BERTIE'S QUEST

Bertie communicated with spirits. They haunted her, drew her forward, and whispered in thoughts and dreams to her; telling her that she had an important purpose for living. She convinced herself that she was divinely chosen to develop Marty into the world's foremost performing actress of erotic romance and films. The Monarch butterfly that landed upon her toe was real. She knew she heard it speak. It was not an illusion. No! It could not have been that! The butterfly had commanded her to use all her abilities. The delicate messenger challenged her. She was to find Marty, the woman with the butterfly tattoo. Then, she was to shape her natural promiscuity into universal recognition and stardom; and thus enable Marty to change the world. Bertie understood that she was on a divine mission:

'I will groom Marty to become the world's most widely acclaimed erotic actress.'

A light bulb switched on in Bertie's mind. It clearly illuminated the goal. The steps needed to make everything happen came into focus. Creating her finished product would require endless persistence and diligence. And that suited Bertie's work ethic perfectly. Other mentors might chastise Marty for her promiscuity, or encourage her to marry a man who could satisfy her sexual needs. A zealot might even try setting Marty on a male-prescribed straightened path of righteousness; but not Bertie. Her inner voice commanded her:

'Never rest until you fully develop and finely polish the promiscuous proclivities of this remarkable young woman.'

Bertie obeyed her mandate. She worked tirelessly to fashion Marty's raw talent and desires. Erotic Romance served up tastefully, beautifully, and steamy hot became Bertie's genre of expertise. She didn't merely knock on that genre's door. She bulldozed it flat. Then she rebuilt and redefined it as INTIMACY ARTISTRY, the ultimate expression of woman's innermost sexual feelings, for appreciation by men and women.

Bertie kicked the antiquated perceptions of pornography to the curb. She ushered in a whole new realm of sensitivity that captured the feelings of women who dared to freely experiment with lovers and love making. Bertie became the Avant Garde creator in her redefined genre's modern era. She weaved breathtaking cinematic intimacy into spectacular feature films, emboldening women's deepest feelings with Marty's performance artistry. She fired couple's imaginations to understand and crave everything that was possible in their relationships. Tireless study and dedicated coaching coaxed perfection from her protégé. Marty's films became cutting edge sexual expansion art, captivating minds, and souls.

Bertie's refocused effort tailored Marty's performances to advance her own vision-quest. Their new films brought Bertie's epiphany to life. Under Bertie's instruction, the younger woman blossomed. She became renowned as the world's most accomplished erotic performer. In film and off stage, Marty became the most highly sought-after sex goddess in modern history. Bertie proudly watched her protégé become the contemporary world's Aphrodite, Helen of Troy, and Venus, all packaged into one living temptress.

Bertie visualized her dream unfolding. The world would open its arms to embrace the spectacular work they did. Everyone would love them both. Marty would be crowned Queen of Intimate Artistry, the renowned and adored film sensation. Marty would earn Academy Awards for best actress; Bertie would win for best film. Together they would shatter all barriers to the free expression of sexual artistry in film.

Men from all corners of the world would throw themselves at Marty's feet. They would be like flower petals strewn on the footpath before a virgin bride. Women would fantasize that their lives could be like Marty's. Many would take up prostitution, striving to be more like Marty. Others would imagine the special wonders of being Marty's lover. Women *and* men would *plead to make love with her; and they would ALL LOVE* her!

When Marty finally held her bouquets of roses, accepting recognition as the world's greatest intimate film actress, she would bow and thank Bertie for making it possible. Bertie visualized all this: The countless hours of film study; technique practicing; emotive expression coaching; position coaching; pelvic, lip, and vaginal presentation experiments; lighting and camera angles; love making position studies; experimentations with partners to create perfect erotic sensations and exacting climactic impressions; perfection of Marty's lips and tongue positions upon cocks' heads and circumcision rings as her hands stroked their shafts and fondled and squeezed their balls; exacting applications of sensitizing stimulations and pressures; eyes flashing tantalizing expressions of ecstasy and erotic euphoria as partners' cocks spurted cum onto Marty's perfectly illuminated tongue; seduction imagery backdrops with pictures of the prankish flute-playing Pan; Marty lying nude on zebra skins with her eyes flashing their divine ecstasy of lust in indelibly explicit moments.

Particularly, Marty's eyes! Bertie understood the young whore's eyes were their greatest asset. She and Marty studied still frames of Marty's eyes for hundreds of hours. Every evolution of her seductions, from initial introductions to final ejaculations would be meticulously examined and critiqued with their focus being on her eyes. Bertie's coaching experience convinced her that fornication scenes were not what enticed Marty's fans to buy her film downloads. It was her eyes! Sex was Marty's steak, but those eyes were the sizzle that sold that steak. Their hints of the devil's persuasive evil, their sheen of immoral naughtiness, and the way they alternately played vixen and helpless innocence tantalized male libidos and set men's' minds to fantasize. And that sizzle! Those hints from her eyes of what might be possible; what might come next, is why women envied her, and what made men go crazy.

Bertie understood that creating piping hot sizzle was the key to sales. So, they studied and practiced to perfect those exact right looks and perfectly timed expressions. Bertie often opined that the way a woman used her eyes could melt a man and capture his heart, even if the woman had the body of a cow.

Marty's eyes became highly trained, expressive eyes. They were windows into her carefree, immoral pansexual mind. And they were exceptional eyes, large, brown irises, trained to flawlessly express sensuous delight behind eyelashes that thirsted for romance and eyebrows that breathed temptation. They made heartbeats quicken and cocks stiffen. They perfectly expressed her joy of accomplishment when her partners achieved ejaculation.

Bertie demanded a particular look that captivated viewers whenever Marty flashed her eyes. It combined ecstasy, intimacy, wholesomeness, and shameless immorality. She demanded that this look capture all those feelings simultaneously. And she understood that that look had to originate from honestly felt feelings within Marty's limbic mind. The challenge was to get Marty to have and express all those feelings simultaneously. The two women worked diligently on Marty's look until they were confident that it would flood viewers' limbic zones and drown all resistance to Marty's siren invitation of lust. Facial muscles were touched and pushed and trained until Bertie knew they had achieved the right setting for Marty's eyes. George and six additional partners volunteered for Marty's felatio practices, spurting their semen onto her triumphant, tantalizing tongue, until the exact expression Bertie wanted became reflexively second nature for her budding starlet.

Bertie demanded other, different looks. She trained Marty's tantalizing eyes to express profound awe and wonder upon beholding a partner's cock for the first time. The eyes were coached to convincingly show heavenly pleasure while Marty achieved her orgasms; flare with carnal delight while her partners' cocks thrusted deeply into her; reveal a mischievous goddess's wicked delights while twerking; savor a vixen connoisseur's evil adoration of her partners' testicles while fondling and sucking them; beckoning with an alluring temptresses' sinful promises while wantonly displaying her cum pool; and incinerating all prudish resistance to cavorting with her, by flashing whoring lust-fired eyes; tantalizing her partners while inviting her viewers to join her; surrender their souls to her; abandon all loves that came before her; and confidently expressing success while drawing her lovers into the bottomless depths of her sinful sexuality; all while simultaneously whispering:

'Come to me now, surrender your soul to me, adore me and the things I will do with you. And above all, love me.'

Bertie paired all those unforgettable expressions with Marty's angelic face. Bertie even taught Marty's face how to speak silently, while it smiled:

'*We both know you want to make love with me. Nothing is stopping you. Don't be afraid. Come closer to me. We both know it will be wonderful.*'

Bertie explained they were actually using Marty's face as their stage in a human morality play. Bertie coached Marty's natural expressions, defining them, making them more convincing and more perfect in every way. Bertie often voiced her adamant belief:

'*A woman's face can message a man to approach her and offer himself up for her seduction without the woman ever uttering a single word.*'

She worked tirelessly to make Marty's face beam seduction's rays; and draw men to her assuring smiles, much as a beacon light guides ships to safety from uncertain seas. Bertie held court on Marty's facial muscles. She touched and held Marty's facial skin and muscles in the exact positions she wanted during all facets of seduction and sexual activity. Bertie trained Marty's face to communicate its predictably consistent, subtle message:

'*I am love.*'

Regardless of how immoral or kinky the sex act by conventional standards, regardless how immoral the scrip dialog, Marty's face beamed confidently to the cameras:

'*My immorality is perfectly normal, acceptable, psychologically healthy, and in complete comportment with my natural persona.*'

If the script called for her to seduce another's husband, her face would never frown or indicate moral doubts about her task. If the script called for her to cheat on her own husband and seduce a stranger, her face would show only joy, but nary a trace of guilt or remorse. In every film, in every scene, her face would assure her viewers that shameless immorality was perfectly normal, acceptable social behavior.

Her angelic face would radiate Marty's pride in every successful seduction scene and her revelry during every orgy. Guilt, shame, equivocation, self-consciousness, and doubt were trained to never appear on her precious stage face; not even for one equivocating second. Bertie succeeded. She established Marty's beautiful face as the poster image of deliciously innocent, carefree, immoral whoredom.

Bertie also trained Marty to coordinate her face, head movements and eye expressions, with her screen entries and exits; and to hold those captivating expressions for the perfect portions of film time. Using George's penis and sometimes dildos with Marty, Bertie practiced tirelessly to achieve those expressive perfections.

Bertie's dogged determination was forceful and relentless. There were many sessions where she worked Marty to exhaustion. Other porn stars had no inkling of the work Marty and Bertie invested into perfecting Marty's craft. They had no one in their camp that shared Bertie's relentless intensity. Meticulously, studiously leaving nothing to chance, Bertie methodically molded her protégé into the world's foremost sex goddess, never doubting she would succeed and never wavering in her commitment to Marty. Bertie's willpower foresaw reality:

'Marty will be the greatest, most famous, adult film actress of all time. I will make it happen.'

It was destiny. Whenever Marty was not on set, at home with Bob, promoting a product that she endorsed, or servicing a Premium Member, she was at Bertie's practicing to achieve perfection. Bertie wanted nothing for herself other than the ultimate satisfaction she craved. She only wanted Marty's recognition and gratitude. Bertie was, in her soul, a giver.

"Marty, how many other performers make you feel like Josh and Marshawn make you feel?" Bertie's question hotly pursued her quest. Her vision drove her to refashion culture, open it to love, especially public acceptance of unashamed, uninhibited embrace

of expressive, explicit sex. She was determined to take public opin-ion by the shoulders, shake it hard and scream:

'Listen! Pay attention! What I'm telling you is important! You are all fucked up out there! You've got everything wrong! Look at what beauty and artistry really is! It is here! Embrace it and love it. Intimate artistry is healthier than violence films, much better for you than neurotic films with actresses performing histrionic gestur-ing, and better for your anger management issues than watching football. Wake up! Watch intimate film artistry. Get a healthier, more loving mind; and the world will be a happier place!'

But, before she could open peoples' eyes to the breathtaking beauty of Marty's work, Bertie needed data. She needed to hear Marty's input. Marty responded by sharing with Bertie, from her premium membership list, the men that gave her those intimate 'feels' that she craved most.

"About six or seven super strong and hard, long-lasting white guys, probably ten beautiful black men who really understand how to make love with a woman; and six special women that drive my libido insane crazy. But I often connect with my women partners even more than my male partners, Bertie. I feel hot blood flushes in my face more with my tongue lovers than I do with cocks. It's a different rush. It's deeper, more inside me and more personal because their minds and thoughts are so closely connected to their tongues.

"You understand, Bertie. You know I love our intimacy. You know how it's different than when we're with a man. It's the sweetest, sweetness love. It's like we're angels confirming to each other that we're sacred vessels of love; that our bodies are sacred, and we can be together, inside our special knowing place. Men can't feel intimacy in the same way we do. It's hard for them to understand."

"Yes, sweetheart, I do know it's different. But I'm reaching for your on-set feelings here. Why Josh and Marshawn, Marty? And

what heats you with the ones you prefer, compared with all your other partners? What causes your heat flush?"

"Oh, gee, Bertie, it's how they are with me. Each one is different, but each has a special way with me. I remember their sexuality; the way they make love with me. I retain their ways in my memory. Then, when I see them again, I get aroused and I flush. I get all excited, knowing I'll be with them. I want to hold them in my arms and make love. Each lover has a particular way of getting into that special place in my mind.

"It's like my mind has doors inside it, and behind each door is the special way a particular man makes love with me. When my thoughts go inside that door, I can remember his ways. I remember our positions, our settings, how I felt, how and when we orgasmed, the things we said to each other, everything. When I see him, his door opens again and those intimate erotic memories flood back to me.

"I can't wait to make love with him again. That causes my face to flush. My flashbacks happen quickly. The many ways we've made love before all run together in my mind; and that gets me excited. I think my nymphomania has a lot to do with it, but I'm not sure. My brain is like an encyclopedia. It's filled with memories of my different lovers and my sexual experiences with them."

Marty's thoughts about Bob came forward into her mind. She remembered the beginning of their affair; how she seduced him. It all flooded back to her. David had ordered her to seduce him so he wouldn't be tempted to leave the Firm with Barbara and do his corporate deals with another firm. They were in the conference room. Bob was at the white board, explaining equations to her. She was bored. She wanted to begin her seduction. That's when she flipped her Ferragamo shoe off, onto the floor. And when Bob picked it up and turned to put it onto her foot, he saw her vagina for the first time. She wore no panties that day.

He was smitten all right. She touched his face with her hand and lifted his eyes to the level of her vagina; and she held him there, letting him know she wanted him. Predictably, her ploy worked beautifully. They agreed to meet at her house later that afternoon. He told her later how much he wanted her; how hard it was to wait those few hours before they made love that first time. And they made love all that afternoon and evening. She played the Ave Maria, over and over. It was spellbinding love. She remembered how impressed she was with Bob's hardness and his stamina. He was unlike other men; extremely passionate; caring; loving. It was all so real. She needed him from that first time onward.

Then, at David's instructions and with all expenses paid, she accompanied Bob as they traveled the country selling the Firm's main product, shares of its Fund. And they made love everywhere and often. From early sunrise on Bar Harbor's Cadillac Mountain, to sunsets on the beaches of Oahu, Hawaii; and New York, New Orleans, San Francisco, and twenty other cities in between, they made love and more love; and they became inseparable.

In Nashville, Tennessee, Marty learned a certain truth about herself. She could not be a monogamous woman. Monogamy as monotonous. While Bob was out selling, she dressed herself to go prowling. And she found a biker's bar. She teased the bikers' interest at the bar; and then she went to the pool table and fucked all five bikers. Oh yes, she fucked them really good. She loved it, too. She came back a second day and fucked all of them a second time.

But then, in the Shenandoah valley of Virginia, she learned a second, contradictory truth about herself. It was after she and Bob had discussed religion. They had decided that the Moses story was about a hot Hebrew girl. Her vagina was the burning bush that made Moses go to Egypt to free the Hebrews; not some actual burning bush. And, her burning bush was the reason why Moses left his gentile wife and kids. He had to have the Hebrew woman; just had to have her.

That's when Marty knew it was safe to confide in Bob. They had made love while looking out from their tent flaps at the Milky Way's blazing path of stars. That's when she revealed her recurrent dream:

"Bob, sweetheart, if we were married, would you always wear my wedding ring? I mean, would you be true to your marriage vows and never take it off?"

"Of course, Marty. I would treasure it. It's a symbol of union. It makes a man complete to have a life partner and a faithful love."

"I'm glad you feel that way. I think of the ring as a symbol of the woman's vagina; and I think of the man's ring finger as a symbol of the man's penis. And I think of the finger through the ring as symbolic that the man's penis will always stay true to his wife's vagina. Do you think I'm crazy to think that way?'

"No, Marty, I think that's a beautiful thought."

"Well, Bob, can I tell you about this recurring dream I have?"

"Sure."

"Okay, well, please don't let this shock you. But I often dream that about fifty men come to me, one after the other. And each man fucks me and ejaculates a huge volume of semen into my vagina. Then, my vagina becomes like this lake, filled with creamy white semen. And then, these fifty men place their wedding rings onto this golden neckless chain and give the chain to me. I then dip the chain of wedding rings into the semen lake inside my vagina; and my semen lake dissolves their wedding rings and their marriages. And after that, all these men's penises belong to me; and I can have any penis I want, whenever and wherever I want it; and I can fuck practically non-stop, forever."

"You really dream that?"

"Yes."

"That's some dream."

"Do you think I'm terrible?"

"No. Do you think you would love fucking all those men?"

"Oh yes, Bob, I do. Honestly, I really would. I'd get this thrill out of knowing that they'd rather have me than their wives. I'd love them for choosing me. I'd tell myself that what I'm doing is right and good; that I'm freeing them from a life they don't want; kind of helping them shake themselves free of their religious brainwashing."

"Have you told anyone else about this dream?"

"Oh yes. I've told my shrink, Mrs. O'Dell."

"I didn't know you had a shrink."

"Oh, I do. And she's wonderful. I think everyone should have a shrink. They help you understand your own thoughts and why your brain comes up with the things it comes up with. Mrs. O'Dell helps me cut through all the religious brain scrambling that my grandmother put me through when I was a little girl. She believes religious schooling of children is very harmful because it puts the concepts of evil and sin into children's minds; and children are naturally innocent."

"So, what does she think of your dream?"

"She thinks it's an effort by my brain to tell me that I need to be more promiscuous. She's told me that I'm naturally promiscuous; and that I should not try to fight my natural tendency. Actually, she thinks I should cultivate my promiscuity and become a porn star. That way, I could fully actualize my innermost need."

"Which is?"

"To make love, Bob. To fornicate."

"Well, we already do a lot of that."

"But she means I should fornicate with many different partners; and that will fulfill my dream, and complete me as a woman."

"I see."

"Well, I have to ask you, Bob. Tell me honestly, would you still love me as you do, if I were to become a porn star?"

"Of course. Yes, I would love you, because I love you. I don't believe I could ever not love you or ever stop loving you, Marty."

"I'm so glad to hear you say that. Then, will you place your hand on my heart, while I place my hand on your heart?"

"Okay."

"And will you repeat after me? I swear, here and now, that my soul will always love your soul, from now until eternity, and for all the different future lives that our souls will know?"

"Yes."

"Good, then swear it. You must swear it, Bob. You must take an oath upon your soul."

"Okay." And Bob repeated the soul oath to Marty.

"That's wonderful, Bob. Now we will be together as one, through all eternity. Now, I need you to learn how to really, really love me. I've made my vagina very clean; and I've scented myself with gardenia and lilac. Now, I want you to place your mouth on my vagina,"

"Okay." Bob did as he was asked.

"Good, Bob. Now, I want you to imagine that the butterfly wings on my tattoo are your wings. I want you to imagine that you are a butterfly and I am a delicious flower."

"Okay." Bob responded.

"Now, I want you to imagine that your tongue is your proboscis. And you are going to use your tongue to locate my clitoris. It's that elongated nub toward the upper portion of my vagina. Place your tongue over it and start rubbing it gently with your tongue."

Bob nodded his acquiescence and began performing cunnilingus, as Marty instructed him.

"That's very good, Bob. Now, I want you to stroke my clitoris with your tongue along each side of it, and over the top of it, lovingly

and gently; and I want you to tongue-tap it every so often, to give it a different sensation of stimulation. Will you do that?"

Again, Bob managed to nod his understanding; and he began performing cunnilingus in earnest.

"Oh, Bob, that's wonderful. I'm becoming highly aroused. I'm going to orgasm shortly. Don't be afraid. I'll convulse a little in my hips and vagina. That's my natural reaction to my tiny vaginal glands releasing their fluids through my vaginal walls. When my fluids flow, I want you to imagine that they are the nectar from the flower you stimulated. And, like a good butterfly, I want you to drink my fluids. Can you do that?"

Bob nodded. Shortly thereafter, Marty came. Her fluids flooded Bob's mouth; and he drank all of them.

"Oh, Bob, that was beautiful," Marty cooed while continuing to press her vagina against Bob's mouth. *"Now, I want you to kiss me. Come up here to my face and kiss me. And I want you to make love to me. I need to make love, Bob. I need to be completed as a woman."*

Bob did as Marty instructed him that day. She remembered the day well. It was after they made love a second time that Bob asked her to marry him and she asked Bob to marry her. They both agreed that they would marry; and Marty threw away her birth control pills.

When she returned to the Firm after the trip to Virginia and Maryland; and after she and Bob had seen the wild horses, and the mares with their foals; and after they made love on the beach at the Assateague Wildlife Refuge, she recalled how she and Bob had promised each other the would have children together. They would be a family.

But then, David found out about their engagement. That's when he blew his stack and fired her. He told her that her instructions were specific. She was to seduce Bob away from Barbara; ruin their budding love affair. And she did that, like the good company girl that she was. But then, David blew his stack and turned beet red. He sputtered and screamed. He raged a temper tantrum like a three-year-old would rage.

"You were only supposed to seduce him and destroy his love for Barbara! You were not supposed to get him to marry you! Get to your desk and clear everything out of it. Get out of my sight, you stupid slut! Get out of this building immediately or I'll call security and have you thrown out. You are fired!"

Now, David's upset seemed a thing of the past. He had calmed down. It seemed they were friends again. And why wouldn't they be? They had similar interests; and their common connection through their murders. She tried not to think about David's upsets. It was so much easier to focus on her porn career. Marty's thoughts left her daydream and returned her to the present. Bertie was very excited, expressing her desire to learn about Marty's compartmentalized mind and how she kept her lovers categorized:

"Please, take me through each one of your lovers. I'd like to know them by name and by method. This will lay the foundation for your future films. It's great material, Marty. I can work with it. I can't wait to work with it."

"Okay," Marty nodded, *"but I have many lovers. Each, man, and woman, is special in a unique way. Let me give them to you as I think about them, Bertie. I want to give them to you when I'm relaxed, so I have good concentration about each partner. Let me explain how I feel about them, one at a time, during our future practice sessions, okay? I'll remember them better if I focus on them as individuals, okay? The way each different partner makes love with me is very subtle. I want to be sure you have the complete picture. I can tell you my feelings about Josh now; and then give you another partner the next time we practice; and another after that, and so on, okay?"*

CHAPTER THREE

My way is to begin at the beginning. (Lord Byron: Don Juan)

JOSH'S FOREPLAY

"Sure, Marty, okay. Well, what is it about Josh, then?"

"It's his gentle hands and his patience. Josh likes to undress me slowly. He'll unbutton my blouse, button by button, while he kisses me; or he'll kiss the nape of my neck, while he unzips my dress. He gets these erotic chills firing all through my nervous system; and I feel my sex getting hot. He makes me want him to take me, right then and there, while we're still standing up. When he has my blouse and skirt off, or my dress off, he likes to bend me over against a bed or a chair. Then, the way he kisses my back turns me into liquid butter. I melt inside, and become anxious to spread my legs for him. I'm ready; but Josh is just getting started. He has these ways of touching me all over my body that let me know he adores me.

"Then, Josh nibbles my ear while he taps his fingers softly along my sides, until his hands find my waist. That sends erotic sensations traveling down my spine right into my vagina; and it animates me, makes me feel like a live wire. I see myself as this rose bush and Josh as a giant stag, with these massive antlers. He's come to me, to my rose canes, to nibble on my rose hips. My nipple buds feel his lips' tender pulls and tugs. They send pulsations down through my canes; through the nerves in my arms and legs; and into the deep, craving roots of my sex. He makes me tremble. I feel my imagination soaring

into the heavens, to this beautiful place. I visualize this huge, magnificent stag with his gigantic penis, mounting me; controlling my body, holding me tightly to him, with his front legs; holding me perfectly in place while he enters me. It's a serene, other worldly moment; a serendipity, blissful, heavenly feeling. I become so electrified and alive I want to hoist my legs and lock them tightly around Josh's hips while I guide Josh's cock inside me. But I wait for him to enter me the way he wants to do it. My blood becomes hot like a fire's heat."

"Oh, my sweet lover," I'll say to myself, "Josh, you don't need to do another single thing to me. Honestly, Josh, I'm so turned on; so hot for you. Let's make love right now. I don't want to wait. I want you right now, right this minute. Please, Josh. Don't make me wait. Come on, baby, let's start."

"But I remind myself that we're on set; and the film is rolling; and my director wants us to show all this foreplay, so I just say: 'Oh, baby,' and 'yes, yes, yes,' and 'don't stop,' and 'Oh, I'm so turned on.'

"Josh, of course, doesn't stop his foreplay. Josh never stops. He loves foreplay. He loves teasing me until I'm insanely turned on and wildly hot to have him inside me. It's sensual torture. I'm being tortured with pleasure, beautiful erotic pleasure.

"Josh continues nibbling on my back. He starts at the base of my neck and moves slowly down from there; tenderly, lovingly, going lower and lower, until he's on his knees kissing me, gently biting me, on the tops of my ass cheeks. This drives me totally nuts. Electricity is shooting through my vagina. It takes all my willpower to obey the director and express my pleasures by mouthing OOOH's and AHHHS. I'm going animal crazy. My heart is beating faster and my breathing is already rapid, like I'm already making love.

"I want to jump up and down and tell Josh to stop, so I can get his penis inside me; and start making love. But I behave. It's so incredibly hard to behave, because I'm feeling white hot inside already. I desperately need Josh to enter me. But Josh continues

playfully kissing and biting my ass cheeks while he slowly peels down my panties. Now I'm getting tortured out of my mind. My panties are this annoying barrier to my sacred treasure. I want them off of me. I'm so anxious to make love. I want Josh to hurry faster; and get my panties off me. By the time he has almost removed them, I am wildly stimulated and hot inside. I can't wait to take his cock inside me. I am going absolutely, totally crazy out of my mind to make love with him. Josh really knows how to get a woman excited, Bertie. No one does foreplay better than Josh.

"When Josh finally peels me out of my panties, he gives my rump teasingly sweet hand slaps. Those slight, stinging sensations send me into an erotic frenzy. They are so highly stimulating. I experience these explicit visions flashing through my mind. I see Josh's penis entering my vagina; watch it sliding all the way into me; and I can feel how it will feel, even before we begin making love. I can't wait to start! I feel my mind telling me that I'm no different than a mink in heat; and I want Josh's penis inside me more than I've ever wanted anything in my life.

"He has perfected his slap touches. I love it! He turns me into a shameless animal when he does that. My inner desires strain to unfold and devour his penis and hold it inside my vagina, forever. Those touches almost make me orgasm before he even enters me! Thinking about what Josh is going to do to me causes me to have a fast orgasm. I can peak very quickly because of his foreplay tech-niques. I totally lose control of my mind; I am so dying to fuck him. It's very hard for me to be a good girl and stay on script.

"I know exactly what Josh will do with me next. It will be so incredibly beautiful! My mind floats away while I'm waiting for him to penetrate me. I'm filled with anticipation. I know he's about to put me in a dream state. His hands open my thighs from behind; and he finds my sex with his tongue. When I feel those initial touches of his tongue, sparklers start dazzling in my head. I've waited so long for

this. I know what he will do next. Josh begins kissing my sex. I feel his passion growing and growing, like he's savoring the juices of a juicy peach. I can tell by how sensitive he is that he loves pressing his lips against my vagina.

"Then Josh performs his ultimate pleasure move. He slides his body under mine. I'm ready for what he's about to do. I run my hands through my hair, trying to contain my desire. But it's no use. I'm on hands and knees; so excited I can think of nothing else, except how wonderful this man is to me; and how beautiful his cunnilingus feels. Josh explores my sex with his marvelous tongue until he discovers my clitoris. I feel like I'm his precious goddess, the love of his life, when he does this. I know sex with this man and his tongue is the best sex I'll ever know in my entire life.

"He's so masterful and artful, Bertie. His tongue strokes my clit like it's a priceless gem; and he's come here to be with me; to worship it. Now my wildness feelings spread from my brain; travel throughout my entire body and flood into my vagina. This wildness feeling consumes my entire body, every single cell that I have in me. I can tell I'm losing all thoughts of everything else, except how pleasurable I feel from what Josh is doing with his loving tongue. I know I'm starting to orgasm. And, I know that, no matter what my director says, no matter how long he wants this scene to run, I want to let myself go. I want to express my passions and explode with an honest, love-filled orgasm.

"Then I feel this new sensation. It's hard to describe. It's like my entire body is suddenly transported to a fantasyland of erotic sex. I can't decide whether to stay on my hands and knees with Josh under me; performing cunnilingus with me; or whether I want to turn around and recline into the missionary position, so I can French kiss Josh and play my tongue all over his tongue while I make love with him. I ask myself; do I want my orgasm to release now, or would it be more loving, more meaningful to Josh, if I came with his penis

inside me so he could feel my passions with his cock, instead of his mouth? I'm stimulated out of my mind, and I'm incredibly hot and slippery wet. I want to run my fingers through Josh's hair; and dig my fingernails into his back when I come. I want my arms holding and squeezing him close to me, feeling his entire body pressing against mine; and with my tongue in his mouth; and his cock deeply inside me. I want to be wild when I come. I want to thrust myself upward, like crazy, to the heavens. I don't even want to slow down to breathe.

"I could make love forever with Josh. That's what his foreplay does to me. He gets me so crazy anxious that he melts me from the inside out. I want to completely submit to him, let my body go crazy while he pleases me in every way imaginable. I'm constantly telling him how good it feels; telling him to keep going; and to never stop; and to come inside me. And I'll be whispering to him, even shouting how much I love making love with him, while the film is rolling. I want to lie under him and lick his balls and suck him, while he leans over me; and stimulates me, using his fingers inside my vagina. And then I want to hold him close and French kiss with him while he enters me. I want to have those experiences with him. I don't want a director's script to take those moments from me. When a girl is in love with a man, like I am with Josh, she doesn't want to be told how to love. She just wants to love.

"I'm already dripping like juicy hot, slippery butter when Josh's penis finally penetrates me. I feel wonderful and completely loved while we make love. There are no words that describe how I feel at that instant when he very first enters me. Something magical happens to my body. There's this realization that our foreplay is finished, but I don't want to let go of it. I don't want it to end. I want Josh to play with my body all over again; and at the same time, I want his penis inside me forever. I don't ever want his cock to be outside of me; not for a single second. Once we start making love, I want him to keep going forever. I totally love Josh and what he does to me. I

*want his touches and his cock always; like I want to be his love slave,
every moment of every day.*

"When the shoot is over and the director says: 'Cut. Wrap it,'
his command brings no joy to my ears. I'm not like many other
porn stars. I don't want to stop. I don't want to leave the set. I'd like
to continue holding Josh, kissing him, stimulating him; getting
him hard again; doing it all over again. Sometimes I find myself
imagining that I'm Josh's special Kittie and he's, my Leo King. I
fantasize that he has a penis barb which hooks me deep inside
my vagina. We become inseparable. We can't uncouple. We're just
stuck together, making love until we pass out.

"I did that last film shoot with Josh at a ranch near Aspen.
That night, after filming, I stepped out onto a patio to breathe
in the fresh mountain air. I looked up at the stars and saw the
entire Milky Way Galaxy. I felt like this huge band of brilliant
stars was looking back at me and telling me something. It was as
if the spirits were speaking to me through the stars, telling me
to feel special and be happy. I remember how happy I felt. I was
grateful to the spirits, and those stars, that I was blessed to be an
uninhibited immoral whore; one who is accepted, adored; and
honored, loved; and paid extremely well for creating explicit,
romantic erotic films. I remember feeling so good about my
life, so happy to be able to make love in so many exotic settings,
with so many handsome and physically well-endowed lovers;
and thrilled that, through my erotica, I was able to connect with
many like-minded women, with whom I had romantic relationships. I couldn't imagine any other lifestyle that would be nearly
as fulfilling as the one I have.

"As I stood there inhaling the sweet-grass smells of freshly
mowed hay, Josh came beside me and put his arm around me. He
didn't need to do that. We were off set and on our own time until
the next afternoon. But by embracing me, holding me close to him

the way he did, he let me know that he cared about me as a human person, not just as a porn star. I put my arm around his waist to let him know I cared for him, too.

"Josh then kissed the top of my head, like I might have been his little sister. I giggled when he did that. Then he started kissing my neck and reaching under my top, touching my nipples with his other hand.

"Josh," I said, "You don't need to be doing that. We're off set now."

"But I want to," he answered. "I love touching you. When I touch your body, I lose my soul to yours. I lost my soul when we were on set today. I want you to take it away from me again. I don't ever want it back."

"Then touch me," My eyes promised my lasting commitment to our sins. I knew Josh loved me, as a woman. I turned to him and clasped him in my arms. "Let's both lose our souls."

"Then I kissed Josh. It wasn't in my contract. I knew I didn't have to kiss him off set, but I wanted to. When we kissed that night on the ranch patio, I fell in love with him. This was real love, not sweetness, porn-set love, but honest 'I love you' love. We didn't know much about each other then. All we understood was that our two bodies loved each other; and we clicked beautifully together while we made film.

"Once we kissed, one thing led to another. Josh began pinching my nipples and fingering me while I stood there, looking up at the stars, breathing in the sweet smells of freshly mowed hay. I loved what he was doing.

"Would you like to stay with me tonight?" I asked him.

"He answered 'yes' to my invitation. We went to my room and got naked. After we got into bed, Josh entered me from my PB position. I felt wonderful sensations everywhere inside me from Josh's huge penis. My fears of abandonment didn't come that night.

I felt secure, as if it was Bob who was there in bed with me. After we made love, Josh and I spooned and nodded off.

"I fell asleep with his huge arms wrapped around me; and the wonderful feeling of his gorgeous huge cock far up inside me. When I awoke, I discovered he had come inside me during the night. I felt wonderful and wholesome, like I was a meaningful part of Josh's life, knowing that he did that; like I might someday be his wife or something. This feeling confused me, because Bob often comes inside me that same way while we sleep together. I wondered if I could live with both Bob and Josh; and whether they'd like taking turns coming inside me while I slept.

"I lay there thinking about asking Josh if he'd like living with us and sharing me with Bob; but I reminded myself that he was leaving for a year to ski and surf; so, I didn't ask him. We made very loving film the next day; but while we made convincing porn love I kept wondering if I'd ever be fortunate to sleep with both Josh and Bob. That's how I knew I had feelings of genuine love for Josh. I'd like to have him in my life every day, forever. I knew I'd fallen in love with him.

"That describes my feelings when I'm with Josh. I'll describe my feelings about another partner at our next session, okay Bertie?"

"Yes, yes, okay. That was more than okay. It was precious and wonderful, Marty. I believe Josh will come back to you; and I believe that Bob loves you so much that he'll share you with Josh, if that would please you. Do other lovers who cause your blood to blush into your skin, the same way it does for Josh, also cause you to have these intense romantic feelings?"

"Well, there are so many subtle differences. I keep my lovers in that encyclopedia in my mind, that I told you about; but, yes, every one of my lovers turns me on in this similar way. I have a genuine heartfelt romantic love attachment to all of them. Honest. I love being romantically in love with all of them."

"Great, we're hitting on something here. I'll search back through all your films and look for that sudden blush in your skin color; then I'll get blow-ups of those frames. I'll create files on each of your favorite partners and your feeling notes about every man and his methods of arousing you. I'll maintain the notes in our PARTNERS FILES. When you feel that hot erotic romance about a partner, we'll identify that partner, by name; and then catalogue your feelings, as you respond to that partner's foreplay and love making methods.

"We'll delve into excruciating, minute detail until we completely understand how each partner turns you on; and we'll document your erotic sensations during foreplay, while you give felatio, while you copulate, and while you give and receive cunnilingus. We'll understand exactly why you feel the feelings you're experiencing from before the filming starts, until after it ends.

"I'll coordinate with our production companies to get only those men who give you the most arousal; the most satisfaction; the greatest tenderness; and the greatest feelings of dominance and submissiveness on your sets. We'll make sure the feelings you are having are exquisitely expressed in your facial, and your eye and body movements. Men and women world-wide are going to experience every conceivable sexual emotion through watching your film work, Marty.

"It will cost more to perfectly capture your romantic feelings, but it will be worth it. You'll see. I saw how your face and body became love hungry and alive when you started kissing Josh. It was totally believable that you love him. There was nothing phony or faked about it. I certainly believed it. That wasn't acting. That was real love, wasn't it?'

"Yes, absolutely it was. I was head over heels in passionate love with Josh while we filmed that erotic scene. I wasn't faking it. I wanted to become romantically involved with him."

"Fantastic! Beautiful! Try to always have expressive feelings like that about every man you partner with, okay? I mean whatever feeling we are trying to capture in a particular scene, whether it's tenderness or whether you're making another woman jealous, whether you're experiencing an orgasmic frenzy with multiple lovers, whatever you are feeling, we are going to capture your feelings to the best of our abilities. You can express those feelings, can't you? I mean you can show feelings of genuine, romantic love with your partners, can't you?"

"Yes, Bertie, of course I can. I can do that because it's true. I love all my partners that way. It's not acting for me. It's just me being who I am. I'd love it if you'd line up the partners I love most, and coordinate my film shoots with the different production companies. It's much easier for me to work with men that heat me up like Josh does, than pretending I feel sexy about someone I haven't met.

"There are those parts in my films where my feelings sometimes need to build, before I can create beautiful intimacy with a partner; but when I'm already hot for my partner; and when my vagina is just dying to start; I'd like to be able to skip that build-up step and just let myself go; be my partner's lover; and begin making love. When I'm mentally into making love before we start filming, it's much more enjoyable. I simply open my mental encyclopedia's door for that partner; and I'm totally ready to make love. We could work on my expressions by studying my feelings with those partners in all sorts of situations. This will be fun! Thank you, Bertie, for showing me how others see me."

"I'll take care of everything, Marty. Trust Bertie on this. No detail is unimportant when we're making you into the top performing adult film star. When you feel love like that toward a partner, we will emphasize that love feeling; and we'll leave those scenes in your films exactly as you create them, uncut. I need to understand everything you think about while you are on the set. We'll get you to first place by serving up an array of unforgettable feelings in every film. Your fans will be amazed! Your films will dazzle them. You'll take their breath away. Your film art will be how people come to know erotic romance. They'll hold images of you in their hearts. Millions will fall in love with you. I promise.

CHAPTER FOUR

The devil is in the details. (Friedrich Nietzsche: Philosopher)

EROTICISM'S DETAILS

"Now George, study carefully the close up of Marty's vagina in this next frame." Bertie's attention turned to Marty's lustrous vagina, carefully scrutinizing it for any detail that might be accented in any way during filming.

"Look how plump and healthy it is, and how it has that beautiful reddish hue from making love. See how beautifully it contrasts with its dark center channel, to its first pink border; then moving outward to more redness; then to her final, outer pink border? Michelangelo couldn't create a sculpture as beautiful as that, George!

"Her vagina is more beautiful and delicious looking than a juicy, freshly ripened peach. It's all meaty and plumped up from being freshly fucked. It's like it has a life and thoughts of its own; like it realizes how gorgeous it is; and it's begging to be eaten. It looks tasty yummy! Connoisseurs of cunnilingual sex can only dream of kissing a vagina that beautiful, George. I can't stop obsessing about kissing it myself, even for hours after I've watched this film.

"Now look closely at her face, George. Just as she finishes pulling her panties up, after fucking her first partner, her second partner arrives. Look at how her face lights up and glows with excitement when her new partner kneels before her and peels her panties right

back down again; all the way to the floor; and how she smiles when he starts rubbing his hand over her vagina. See that?

"Did you observe her facial expression as she kicked her panties away? Were you able to catch that? There's a self-awakening happening inside her. Marty has a natural Pavlovian response. Did you see it? It expressed itself in her broadening smile. It's that rush joy of sudden happiness radiating from deep within her. It's her body knowing she's about to have sex again. You're watching a rare phenomenon, George. Her nymphomania is overwhelming all her senses. It's taking control of her.

"Now look again, closely, when this new partner begins licking her vagina. See how her facial muscles relaxed? Can you feel how thrilled she is, by that glow from her face; realizing her new partner is starting cunnilingus; and how she gratefully welcomes his tongue touches to her vagina? She has no desire to stop and rest between partners, George. That's very uncommon. Enjoying erotic romance is Marty's natural state of being, George; and these frames illustrate it. She's unique in her behavior this way, George.

"See how joyous and relaxed her smile becomes while her partner spreads her vagina with his fingers, and cups his mouth to her? See how she arches her back; and how she throws her head back; and how she reveals to her viewers her beautiful open-mouthed smile, George? That's the perfect expressive feeling of a woman enjoying her orgasm from oral sex, George. She pulls my imagination right into her sex, like I'm experiencing those same tender tongue touchings with her! She's naturally unashamed and uninhibited about having her orgasm, George; like she's enjoying her natural God given right!"

"Yes, Bertie, I see what you mean." Ever compliant George nodded his agreement.

"Now, these next frames were shot after that beautiful orgasm, George. See her delightful, playful smile as she takes down her partner's pants? Can you imagine yourself standing there with her? Can

you imagine that that huge beautiful penis is yours, George? And can you fantasize that you are offering it to her for the very first time? Look how her beaming, anticipatory smile breaks out when she takes that gorgeous penis in her hands; just before she places her mouth over it.

"She loves sucking cocks, George. That delightful happiness in her eyes tells you exactly what's in her mind. Those eyes speak volumes. She's relishing the thought of having that cock in her mouth. She's going to love giving head to that penis, and having it ejaculate into her mouth. When she's doing two or more partners at the same time, her pleasure and lust for their penises leaps right from her eyes, and into your heart. I've NEVER seen another woman create erotic feelings like that. Her uninhibited immoral purity creates adoration for her shamelessness, and a heartfelt sense of awe. Viewers love her. They know they're beholding a goddess enjoying her carnal pleasures. Some call what she does 'sin.' But connoisseurs of explicit, erotic art consider her performances magnificent and beautiful.

"She makes people feel HER feelings, experience HER orgasms with their own; and when she performs with multiple partners like she often does, her viewers become even more empathetic. She loves fucking and sucking more than any other adult actress. She's completely comfortable and natural in her role. Her performances are getting better, more loving, and more expressive with every new film she makes, George. She's so incredibly beautiful; so artful; so adorably sensual in the way she goes about her performances. She provides mouth watering salacious whoring and makes falling in love with her so easy; so compelling. She's producing divinely erotic artistry, George. I KNOW what we have here.

"This is MARTY'S time, George. Everyone is leery about going to prostitutes now. Everyone is fearful about wretched pathogens being spread in crowded theaters. Still, people need their vicarious escapes from the harsh realities of the uncertain times we live in.

"Our challenge is to expand Marty's market reach. Years ago, people wouldn't admit that they watched pornography. Many still won't admit it. But they DO watch it, George, they DO! The tracking numbers don't lie. They watch it on the internet. And, they love watching it; but they are still reluctant to admit they love watching it. We're going to change that, George. We're going to rebrand porn into something people consider beautiful, desirable, and acceptable. We're going to make our intimacy art so compelling that people will freely admit that they love watching it. We'll liberate them; make them want to share their experience of watching Marty with their friends; just like they once talked about the Oscars. We're going to get word of mouth advertising going; get intimacy art perceived as the ultimate in haute culture. We'll make the demand for Marty's erotic films explode! Every new film she releases will be a 'must see!'

"Our goal is to fully capitalize on the times we are in. We're not going to call Marty's work pornography anymore. We're creating a new, more desirable venue. We're rebranding Marty's films; calling them 'MARTY'S INTIMATE FILM ARTISTRY,' George. We're going to make watching Marty's films not only acceptable, but Avant Garde, high brow cache! We'll work hard to get people everywhere talking about Marty's latest films; critiquing all the explicit details of every scene she does; getting her more eyeballs than the President's press conferences. We'll make them more interested in her latest film than their week-end football games; more topical to their conversations than their siblings or their friends. We'll make her into a sensation.

"We'll reprogram Americans to think with their limbic zones. Their minds will turn off violence, histrionics, and convoluted plots; basically, everything that encroaches on the mind's limbic functions; get them to toss out all the garbage they watch now. We'll train the population to think only of sex, George! We'll do this by flooding the world with Marty's erotic films and photos. People will see Marty *everywhere; and they'll think of her and her sexual escapades con-stantly. We will attract millions of men, AND women, to Marty and the sensuality she represents."*

Bertie's enthusiasm for her new life's mission was boundless. Under her watchful direction she was convinced Marty could attract legions of adoring followers. She visualized hoards of men, lonely men, lecherous men, adulterous men, and voyeuristic men all pining for Marty; and all of them buying her films. And, women too! Personal attentiveness to perfecting Marty's girl-girl film art would be a delicious extra bonus for Bertie and her closest friends.

She enlisted ever dutiful George to help her mold her new, spirited human clay into the focal point of concupiscent lust. Afi-cionados of the new Modern Morality Standard flocked to Bertie's human creation. Her relentless drive pushed Marty, refusing to be satisfied until she polished her into a world-wide sensation; alone on her pedestal; the rightful recipient of the Gold Medal; not for figure skating and it's limited following; but for intimate artistry and its vast world-wide audience. Bertie reshaped and molded Marty into the world's most desirable woman.

"This is how we'll make certain it happens, George," declared a breathless Bertie, *"We're going to get her the best directors; the best performing partners; and we're going to get her the very best screen writers. We'll place her in the most exotic romantic settings with the best musical scores; but most of all, we'll focus on Marty.*

"She'll always look her freshest, most beautiful self; always be dressed to the nines; always wear the perfect make up; and always have every scene staged and lighted flawlessly. Marty will see the best dermatologists, and the best plastic surgeons. We'll perfectly remove every sunspot, every blemish tag on her body; and we'll perfectly apply electrolysis to every follicle of unwanted hair. Her body will be one perfectly smooth, silky creamy-white living sculpture. Her face will even more stunning than a perfect porcelain doll face.

"Marty's image will be so endearing and classy that everyone who sees her work will dream of her; long for her; willingly turn their guts inside out to be with her; and surrender their fortunes to her; if only they could. We'll make her vagina the most photographed centerfold in the entire world, George. It will always look creamy white and pink; juicy tasty; plumped up; delicious to savor; and anxious to make love. The masses will salivate at the mere thought of her, George. We're going to make them scream for more of her!

CHAPTER FIVE

Now then, it is no more that I do it, but sin that dwelleth in me.

For the good that I would, I do not; but the evil which I would not, that I do. (Two passages from Romans, iii)

ROMANS, ALL

"We're going to position Marty's intimate films as mainstream and acceptable art forms, George. Mothers will dream that someday their precious daughters, if they dedicate themselves to a career in intimate artistry, will perhaps also attain heights of fame and fortune by following in Marty's footsteps. We are riding a tidal wave of societal immorality, George. And we are going to harness it!

"As America's immorality mirrors the late Roman Empire's and while Americans' sexual norms comport with those practiced in eighteenth century Parisian salons, Marty will emerge as the leading persona of the Modern Morality Standard. Her film art, her openly immoral lifestyle, and her sexual escapades will titillate and fascinate the masses. The hard times and the disease scourges already have people believing God has failed them. It's a stage set for easy sales, George.

"Her salacious behavior will be applauded. She will receive honors for her breathtaking wantonness. When she captivates new lovers and takes them away from their mates, the masses will praise her escapades. They'll praise her sexuality. The masses will love Marty for her immorality; and the many scintillating ways she presents it,

George. They will toss aside their traditional morality; and they will positively love her! We're going to make the whole world fall in love with this woman, George.

"Mark my words, George, when we finish polishing Marty's image and add more finesse to her film art; whenever she hooks her legs around a partner, and pulls his cock deeply into her thrusting, sex craven vagina, she's going to pull millions of viewers out of their miserable drudgery and thrust them into her world of limitless mouth-watering sin. She will net new followers by the millions, George. We're going to make immorality beautiful and mainstream, George. We're going to trademark Marty as the symbol of purest, everlasting immorality. People will love her immoral ways more than they ever loved their religions or their relatives.

"We can achieve this because times have changed, George. People are stressed. They are depressed. Nothing works for them. They are giving up on religion and losing hope. We'll help them discover the escape they need. We'll give them something to believe in again. We'll refashion the very concept of adult films as we rebrand Marty.

"People will stop seeing love making as something dirty that needs to be kept hidden. Religion has made sex something to feel guilty about, George. We'll make people understand that that kind of thinking is outdated and ridiculous. We'll return morality to the way it naturally was, before religion distorted it. People will see how splendid love making can be, George. We'll fashion the world's most beautiful, lascivious, sensational whore into a deity. We'll refashion Marty's promiscuity and present it as divine art, George. She'll become a goddess.

"I cannot coach what Marty brings to intimate artistry George. I can't. She has this inner beauty that comes alive and glows while she has sex. She's so beautiful and wholesome, she's beyond fantastic, George. She endears and captivates. She draws out the imaginations of viewers' minds and shows them what's possible. She captures their *hearts, by creating a captivating art form that's more riveting and spellbinding than any Picasso or Rembrandt. She helps people appreciate how beautiful human sexuality is, George. Her fans internalize her love of sex; and they apply it to their own lives. They love her for it.*

"We'll brand the beauty of human sexuality and use Marty's face for the cover of our brand, George. I can't stop gushing over her. I adore her. I'm beyond crazy about her, I love her. She's a godsend. She is life, George. She understands that the purpose of life is to live it. She knows what happiness is; and she lives it so beautifully with everything life has to offer. She represents life and happiness for so many people, George, and for both of us! We're blessed to have her in our lives."

Bertie's discerning eye was approving Marty's honest natural smile during cunnilingus. She assured herself that Marty loved oral sex. Nothing she saw seemed faked or forced. *"That's our Marty, George. She's our perfect angel! Such a gorgeous loving face! I want to hold her face in my hands and kiss it everywhere. Oh, God, I do love her face, don't you love it, George? It's the picture of wholesome goodness and happiness. Look at how she smiles in that frame, George. It's like she's silently calling to the viewer to come and make love with her. Her facial expression in that frame makes me feel intimately close to her.*

"That frame is one we had blown up for our bedroom wall, Marty. When I stare at that picture my sex gets all wet; and then I anxiously dream about your next visit to us. You love having your vagina kissed, don't you, baby? You feel happy when we do that with you, don't you, sweetheart? She's smiling at me and nodding her head, George. Our baby is very healthy and happy, George. Aren't you Marty?"

Marty embraced Bertie and the two women French kissed, as if to confirm their mutual attraction. *"George, sit next to Marty, and put your arm around her. Hug her close to you. She's part of our family now. She's, our baby. You treat her that way, George. Make sure she always feels cared about and loved."*

George obeyed, placing his arm over Marty's shoulder.

"That's better. Now, you feel closer to her, don't you George? Isn't that better? I want all of us to be together and happy." George nodded. He looked at Bertie while wiping a tear from his eye. He understood Bertie's grief had caused her bizarre behavioral turn. He accepted his spousal duty to indulge her. Consorting with the comely tart compensated.

"And, George," Bertie's voice was the one she used when she was about to broadcast her authority, *"The other day, while you and your buddies were at the club playing eighteen holes, I invited their wives over to watch this same film with me."* Bertie turned and addressed Marty. *"We sat here on the bed and studied your work, Marty. I wanted to get the word out to some ladies whom I know would appreciate your talents, dear. I want to help your career along as best I can. They all think you are the most gorgeous sexpot they've ever seen. They are totally supportive of your work. We're behind you one hundred percent!*

"The other night George and I also had mixed couples over to watch compilations of your films. One of my friends commented that she stopped counting your lovers when she reached one hundred. She wondered if you actually loved all of them; and, if you don't actually love them, why does it appear that you do? I didn't have an answer for her. Could you help me?"

"Oh, gladly Bertie," said Marty,

"Bob is my only true love; but I do have other loves; and my work demands that I appear to love sex, which, obviously, I do. The reason my films are so successful is pretty straightforward. You see, when I'm on set performing, I'm not thinking about myself. I'm thinking about the man who is my partner. Everyone who buys my films already knows I'm an adult film star with my reputation of being an

iniquitous home wrecker and an immoral whore. Most people consider me sacrilegious, pro- abortion, pro-divorce, and shamelessly promiscuous; yet, they still pay money to watch me make love. So, for my film performances I only need to be my natural, nymphomaniac self. But, that's not enough to make the film a raving success.

"My male partner also needs to perform like he truly loves me. That's a very difficult role for most men to play. They are basically unknown actors. The men do not make nearly as much money as I do for the roles they play. Most producers figure men with pricks come a dime a dozen; and, basically, that's true, they are inexpensive actors. People pay to see the woman. They crave her naughtiness; her pleasure while being immoral, sinful. Yet, to make the viewers believe that the man really loves me so that the two of us appear to actually be in love, which is key to creating a smash hit film, I must make that man believe he actually does love me, if only for that hour."

"Keep talking, sweetheart, and don't mind me. I'm listening carefully to every word you are saying," said Bertie. She was on her knees in front of George, sucking and stroking him toward ejaculation. Every so often she looked up at the film to give her comments.

"Sure, Bertie, it's perfectly all right. You're doing great with George. You're beautiful to watch," giggled Marty as she continued. "Men have neuroses, just like women do; but men's come from a different mind set. They have differently wired brains and different hormones.

"While I believe my films are beautiful works of loving art, my partner may think film performing is simply work. Although I profoundly love being a sex worker and I believe that adult film artistry offers a wonderful career path for me, my male partner may have hang ups about making love with me for all sorts of psychological reasons. He needs to overcome those hang ups if the two of us are

going to make a successful film. I don't have time, on set, to figure out what's in his head; so, I need to assume a lot of different possibilities could be at work in his mind.

"He may have been conditioned by his parents or by his religious upbringing that prostitutes are somehow bad women; and consorting with one of us is bad; possibly a terribly evil thing, which will sentence him to an afterlife in hell. He may be impressionable and easily swayed to believe that women who have strong independent personas, like myself, are modern day witches. It's a psychological thing. It can express itself as a guilty feeling in some men. It's wrong-headed thinking. It's only one step removed from the belief that there were witches in Massachusetts' Salem Colony.

"In the years sixteen hundred ninety-two and three, some Salem women were burned to death because of a huge misunderstanding; but that psychology about evil residing in women who choose to live independent lives, persists to this day. This is problematic for some men when they realize that every one of my films will earn me hundreds of thousands of dollars; possibly millions of dollars, over its lifetime; while they are only paid a one-time payment of a thousand or two thousand dollars. Thus, he may subconsciously feel that he's morally damning himself; and also making a financial fool of himself by consorting with me.

"His psychology may have been influenced by a lifetime of force-fed male propaganda. He may hear his head telling him that he's not making a beautiful, sensitive movie, with a morality theme underlying it. Instead, he may think he's simply fucking and performing cunnilingus with an immoral whore; and that he's going to be labeled as unclean or dirty. He may need to be my film partner to get some quick money; but underlying his stated enthusiasm for the work, he may be suppressing revulsion and resentment.

"Many men have great difficulty accepting a woman as their sexual equal, who has the same or even greater requirements for

pleasure as the male. Many men can't begin to understand those deep depths of a woman's sexual needs; and they don't want to learn about those needs, either.

"My partner may possibly have a wife or girlfriend. He may need to make extra money which he's trying to keep secret from her; or, he may have parents who would disapprove of what he's doing. Being caught with me might risk disinheritance; or, he may have buddies at his fraternity house or workplace who will razz him. He may even be a professional. Being seen with me could cost him his medical or legal practice. Are you starting to see the pernicious effects of our male ordered world? Are you getting how that world tramples freedom?

"My films are archived and played for years; so, my partner also runs the risk that sometime in the future someone will recognize him and out him. He could jeopardize his chance to ever get a job as a federal judge; a tenured professor; or a respected religious leader. While I'm very proud of being an internationally renowned whore, happily promoting my fame; he may have opposite life time goals. Most men have very different goals than a career in intimate art-istry; although, I could see, with broader acceptance of the genre, that could change. Perhaps a man with the acting fame of a Richard Burton, John Wayne, or Clint Eastwood will, someday arise in the genre of erotic romance. Who knows? I hope so. That would change perspectives. Until then, my partners' roles may be limited to hav-ing a little naughty fun; making some quick money and remaining anonymous.

"Thus, my task is to help my partner get beyond his neurosis and get him to completely lose himself in love and lust for me; even though he knows it's probable that he'll never be called to perform with me again. It's normal for producers to seek new, fresh faces to act in new, fresh scenes with me. After all, if I was fucking the milk-man in my living room one week; and performing felatio with a pilot

in an airplane cockpit the next week, it wouldn't be credible for the fans to see me with the same man playing both roles; but it's very believable for a world-renowned, notorious whore to make love with both men, as long as their roles are played by different actors.

"So, it's up to me; not the male, to make sure our film succeeds. My porn rankings and my membership business are both at risk, every time I perform. I must make a sensational film every single time. My career depends on it. So, to help my male partner get his mind into the present; and not think much about the future, I do several things.

"Before we even start filming, I complement him on how handsome he is; even if that's not true. I compliment him on how beautiful his penis is; how large it is; how much I look forward to sucking him and fucking him; even if what I'm saying is a white lie. But, that's actually pretty rare. My producers mostly select very handsome, well-endowed partners. So, I'm being totally honest when I tell them I'm anxious to fuck and suck them. That is absolutely true. I love discovering how a new partner makes love. I always learn something, from every new partner. That newness of the experience always excites my curiosity.

"Usually, the producer chooses males that have exceptional penises. Many of my partners have had enlargement surgery; and, at the minimum, they are protein and vitamin E filled; and they have taken their little male erection pill. That keeps them full and hard for over an hour; and, they usually have not ejaculated at all during the previous four days; so, their prostates are packed to overflowing with semen. Thus, their cocks are eager and primed to be milked by my mouth and vagina.

CHAPTER SIX

The danger chiefly lies in acting well; no crime's so great as daring to excel. (Charles Churchill: Epistle to William Hogarth)

LOVE'S TRADECRAFT

"I believe this is vital to making a film successful: I always French kiss my partner and embrace him closely off-set, before we film. I'm not paid to do that; and my partner knows I'm not getting paid for it; but it makes my partner believe I'm eager to make love with him. I also rub his cock through his pants while I press against him. Stimulation dispels inhibition. Toying with my partner's penis, before we start, just makes good sense.

"Men always do what their penises want them to do. I know that. It's the males' greatest vulnerability. I tell my new partner that I can feel myself falling in love with him and I'm hot to get started. I make sure I've given him a good taste of my fresh, clean mouth. He's received stimulation from my searching hands and probing tongue, before the lights and cameras even turn on. If a wife or girl friend has recently kissed him, I want to chase all thoughts of her from his mind BEFORE we start filming. I only want him thinking about fucking me.

"Once on set, I quickly get into a certain mind set; and I keep my mind focused throughout the filming. I must feel emotional love for my partner, even if I do not genuinely love him. I do that by mentally transmitting certain thoughts to him. I appreciate the risks he's

taking with his life to perform with me; and I want him to feel good about it. I tell myself that he'll get the greatest fellatio, and the greatest sex he'll ever have, in his entire lifetime. I mentally communicate that thought to him with every movement of my body; every caress; and every stroke of his penis with my mouth or vagina.

"When I lie down in my missionary position and spread my legs to display my vagina and my butterfly tattoo, I also mentally tell him that I'm opening myself to his love. As I open my arms to him, he sees I am welcoming him as a person, not just as a penis. I mentally communicate that I'm eager to wrap him in my loving arms and legs; and hold him against my lust-crazed body.

"When we lie together, I always hold his face close to mine. When I know his eyes have entered my deep dreamy pools, I touch my lips to his. I want him to imagine how supple they'll feel while I suck his penis. I'm putting his mind through a mental cleansing process. I'm ridding his mind of extraneous thoughts. I know how important this phase of love making is, so I take my time. I rub the back of his neck and stroke his penis while I French kiss him again. I bring the Zen of our souls closer to each other; like we are the only two people in the world; the only two that matter. I reinforce my feelings of sincerity and love for him. When I sense he believes me and trusts his own feelings of desire to make love with me, I know I've purged all other women, wives, girlfriends, and other erotic film actresses from his mind. I know that the only woman living in his mind is me.

"While we are making love, I tell myself that he's special to be willing to perform with me. I never think of myself during that hour. If I thought about myself, I know his mind would sense it. Intimacy is like that. It's the giving of one's self. If his mind thought I was thinking of me, and not him, that could ruin everything. That's why I only think of him.

"I want him to taste my lips and remember my passionate French kisses. I want him remembering feeling my tongue exploring

his. I want him remembering how I loved sucking his cock, from the second my lips touched its head until his semen spurted onto my tongue; and I want him remembering how I lovingly sucked his penis's head, long after he ejaculated.

"I want him remembering how beautifully we made love. That's why I frequently kiss him, and reassure him that he's pleasing me. It's important that the male thinks he's a champion lover. Kissing him frequently reinforces that confidence he needs and helps him perform at his optimum. It's like having the right motor oil in an engine.

"Viewers' imaginations are fired when they see my pelvis and vagina moving in rhythm with my partner's cock strokes and the theme of music. That helps put their minds into the film with me. I facilitate that transference and empathy process. I participate fully with my partner by lifting my pelvis upward with his thrusts; so that his penis stimulates my clitoris during his downward plunge cycle; and also, by rolling my pelvis slightly downward, during his outstroke movement. By moving that way my clitoris always receives maximum stimulation. Thus, I'm highly sensitized; and very likely to climax at, or nearly at, the exact same instant my partner ejaculates inside me. Having that simultaneous orgasm with me boosts my partner's ego. It helps him perform at his optimum, even during, and after, his ejaculation. It's in those after-moments that viewers notice convincing serenity on my partner's face, because the pleasures he's receiving do not end with his ejaculation. They transcend that moment and become a more convincing type of intimacy, one that binds his soul to me as well as his body.

"Our motion should be performed much as a beautifully orchestrated symphony. My most successful films are these visualized, melodious harmonies of my partner penis in rhythm with my vagina. Importantly, I never stop love making with the ejaculation into my vagina. I hold my partner tenderly after he shoots. I kiss him and cradle him with my arms and legs. That takes his mind back to

his infancy and the love he received from his mother. All men crave that feeling of trusting intimacy. I continue rhythmically performing my pelvic stimulations; and, mentally giving him my most loving feelings, loving him even more than before. It's my way of expressing gratitude for who he is, and what he just did with me. He senses that. It stimulates him to continue performing enthusiastically, adoring me, and pleasing me even while he's still releasing semen.

"That's when he surrenders all his love. Often, my partner collapses into me. My fans sense that that is his final moment. My performance creates a "bravo" effect for them, similar to how the matador pleases the crowd when his sword finally pierces the heart of his bull. It's the moment when my fans know I've completely finished my partner.

"I NEVER hurry my man. I rub my hands through his hair while he comes inside me. I often moan OH and AH with pleasure. I softly whisper "yes" and "that's right;' and 'oh, that feels so good, baby;' and 'you're amazing;' and 'I love how you feel inside me;' and, 'I love how you're making me feel;' and, 'That's it. That's perfect. Yes, yes," many times during sex.

"I smile loving and appreciative smiles to him for the beautiful way I feel while we make love. I French kiss him and give endearing nibble kisses to his face and neck, chest, and shoulders. I try to make his limbic zone become crazed over me by the ways my vagina moves and writhes in rhythm with the music and his penis. This effect takes place inside his mind. There, I create the sensation of unforgettable lust and passion. I steadily build his intensity. In the final seconds leading up to and during his ejaculation I can sense his ardent devotion. During this phase, some men have actually told me they were willing to die for me. Whenever I sense that devotion feeling, I know that the film will be wildly successful. I know my fans will feel the same passions they witnessed my partner feeling on their

screens. People are very empathetic and sensitive. They appreciate erotic romantic love when it's beautifully presented.

"I make every partner believe he's, my king. I impart to him that he is special. If, ten or twenty years from now, he's married to some other woman; I want him remembering me, while he makes love with her. My lips, my nipples, my vagina, my soft skin, and my loving embraces and kisses are the memories I want fixed in his mind, forever. After all, he can still buy my films!

"Someday his significant other may discover his past. While they make love she may wonder: 'Does he think of HER lips when he kisses me, HER skin when I lie naked with him, HER vagina when I make love with him? Does he love me, or does he love her? How can he not love her, after the two of them made love like they did on that film? Am I as desirable as she was when they made that film?'

"I'm making passionate love while I'm having these sorts of thoughts because I conscientiously do everything I can to make the film succeed. The most important part of that process is keeping my mind in the right place. That's why I get so intense on camera. You hear my screams of pleasure. And you hear my shout outs to my partners, to do more of whatever it is that they are doing that pleases me. I often get unashamedly explicit. That intensity may cause relationship problems for my partners and the women they are involved with; but I can't help that. My only intent is to make passionate, sincere love so our film succeeds. It's strictly business.

"Bertie, you asked me if I loved these men. Yes, I do. And no, I don't love them in the same way love is meaningful for most people. I appreciate that they are willing to make love with me, which will enhance my career, finances, and fame; and I'm grateful that they'll help me satisfy my nymphomania during that hour of filming; but I do not feel sincere romantic togetherness with them. It's not like my closeness feelings for Bob or Carl. It's somewhat similar to my

feelings for Josh and Marshawn; and several of my other regulars in the Premium Service; and a few others I keep in my mental dictionary; but it is nowhere near as intense or caring.

"It's not the same kind of love a woman has when she has shared meaningful life experiences with someone. It's more of a manipulative love. I call it 'Sweetness love.' That's love making with an immediate financial goal in mind. It's like eating a big piece of chocolate cake with gobs of icing on it. It sends my emotions sky high for the moment; but then the sugar high falls off and crashes, leaving me feeling empty and anxious to make love with someone new. That afterwards time is when my nymphomania craving comes alive and reasserts itself.

"Making an erotic film also causes after effects. Male partners often contact me through the film production company, seeking to strike up a personal relationship. Some ask to meet me for a coffee; others offer dinner; some send me flowers with their card and phone number. Some have even sent notes telling me no other woman or adult film actresses, wives, or girlfriends, ever created feelings of intimacy like they had with me; and some tell me how they lie awake nights, even weeks and months after we've performed; and they can't sleep because they can't stop thinking of me and how much they want to kiss my vagina again; things like that. They actually write stuff like that.

"It's all very flattering, and I know they are sincere and mean well; but I never follow up on those invitations. I can't afford the time to become involved with them. They simply don't have enough money to make a relationship with them worthwhile for me; and, as good as our sex might have been on set, the production companies have endless supplies of handsome, desirable men willing to make a film with me. So, I don't need involvements with performers who aspire to have free sex outside of their contracts.

"My nymphomania cravings increase, too. That's the inescapable after-effect I feel from making erotic films. The more I make love, the more I desire doing more of it. It's a self-reinforcing cycle. It makes me feel that I absolutely MUST make love; and when I'm not making love, I can't imagine any another reason to exist. As soon as I feel my partner's hot cum flowing into my vagina, I notice this stealthy anxiety. It begins rising within me. I get anxious. I try reassuring myself that I'll soon make love again. Shrinks have told me I have obsessive compulsive disorder behavioral symptoms. Some told me to think about something else. But I can't.

"Mrs. O'Dell says I have the classic neurotic symptoms of a nymphomaniac. My nymphomania disorder controls my feelings. My most memorable, highly rated film performances occur when the production companies set up several films for shooting, one or two days apart. I feel happiness knowing that my sex cravings will be satisfied fairly soon. That relaxes me while making a film, because I know I won't have to suffer without sex for lengthy times between films.

"After a shoot, I sometimes feel a little tired; but after eight hour's rest my craving for sex returns. It's automatic, like a stomach getting hungry. It's just there. If I have no shoots scheduled, I'll meet my private service clients during those interim days. I'll normally have six one-hour sessions with private members in the twelve hours after I've rested. The members do not tax my strength like my film partners, but they help control my cravings until I get back on set."

George groaned softly. Bertie had worked her magic. He was ejaculating into her mouth. After they finished, Bertie got up and sat between George and Marty. *"Thanks   for helping us understand how you manage to perform so spectacularly, Marty,"* Bertie sighed. She hugged her protégé and kissed her cheek. Her other hand continued working. She squeezed George's balls and softly stroked him. He was reclined, lying on his back, smiling; lost in thoughts of times and a relationship past:

'Oh Amanda, my dear child, why did you have to leave us? You were the goodness that held our family together. Now you are gone. What are we doing? Where are we going from here? Bertie believes she is being directed by some spirit; but to what end? She seeks to do well by Marty; be her benefactor; exalt her as if she were a deity. There is a sense of madness in our purpose here. And we do not know Marty's soul.

'The young whore is clever. I notice she never takes up a political thought. She hears me and Bertie, and no doubt others, rail about the endless encroachments of government; how the government waxes fatter, and the people's freedoms are diminished, year by year. Marty never takes part in such discussions; but that is not because she doesn't observe things; nor is she stupid. She sees the leftists and rightists tug upon the centrists; both factions pulling the fabric of society apart. She feels the same frustrations that we feel; of that, I am sure. But she wisely takes no side, for there is no percentage in it for her.

'Instead, she targets a weaker woman's marriage and destroys it by taking the woman's husband from her; and then she crows about her destructive deed. She elicits others to heap scorn on the defeated woman and her shattered family. Why? Because Marty understands that the frustration people have about their overall dilemma needs to have an outlet. They know they cannot fight the government. They are too disorganized. They have guns, but they are just the public's placebo, a joke. They have no organization; no leadership. Their frustration simply simmers and mounts. Marty is smart. She gives them their outlet. She satisfies their cravings and helps them vent their pent-up fury.

'What could be more natural than for all the members of that downtrodden, aimless mob to pick upon the weakest one of them;

the hapless, defeated woman? Cleverly, Marty redirects the mob's pent-up angst and turns it into fury against her victim. Cleverly as well, she instructs the mob to blame the displaced wife for losing her husband and family.

'Very pagan-like, Marty harnesses their wrath and shapes it into glory for herself. She portrays herself as the poor oppressed husband's rescue goddess in an imaginary 'survival of the fittest' contest. She is not unlike those desperate men who boxed their pugilistic art during the Great Depression. Barbaric, bloody, repugnant; yet splendid and purposeful. People need to exalt a champion; someone they can idolize who takes their minds off their miseries and gives them hope. Marty is the female version of a Joe Lewis or a Jimmy Braddock. She's the peoples' champion. Marty understands this aspect of her popularity.

'She is, to her followers, much like a beautiful, glorious swan; but she has the morals of a barnyard pig. She has Bertie taken in. It remains to be seen whether she is on board for Bertie's vision; or whether she is merely using Bertie; and me. But why should I care? Amanda haunts my soul. I've lost my dear child. What purpose is life for me now? Without family, without seeing her graduate, marry, have children; share life's moments with her, what reason can there possibly be for me to even live? Amusements abound, but without family, there is no purpose in them; not for me. So, I resign myself to humor Bertie. I'm along for the ride on this. No doubt, the sex will be good; but what purpose does it serve? Marty is not Amanda. That fiction exists only in Bertie's mind, poor woman.

'And, so we embark upon this errand to create a sex goddess who foreswears children and family. For what purpose? Ah, yes, to have manipulative power over others; persuade them to buy more of Marty's pornography. That makes us no different than a vacuous soul who wears a political suit. Perhaps something good will come of all this? Perhaps Marty will have an epiphany and decide to have a husband, a child, and a family? And all will be wonderful; and we will have played some small role in it. We shall see; but we do not have that now. And so, I go along for my ride on this little game these two women play; to observe life; to hope for a meaningful purpose in it all. And, meanwhile, the sex will be good.

'Amanda, my dearest, sweet Amanda; forgive me. I have failed you as a father. I never did enough with you. I never spent enough time with you. We didn't go sailing or horseback riding nearly enough; we didn't go to enough plays together and discuss them afterwards; nor did we go on enough walks together or play enough board games together. I was not strong willed enough to stop Bertie's madness as she molded you into your Olympic form. I didn't put a stop to her madness when you broke your wrists and arms trying to perform to her standards. I am so terribly sorry, Amanda.

'And now, I must confess to you that I am about to become the worst father possible. You see, the ties that bind our souls together are being severed. Marty wields the razor-sharp knife of sexual lust; and it cuts deeply into my memories of you, dearest daughter. Her evil soul is very possessive. She has a narcissist's soul; and it demands all of me; and it steals away my thoughts. I feel it. Her soul is pulling my soul into her bottomless abyss; causing me to lose my morality, and my own soul.

'I can't do this any longer, Amanda. I can't relive those moments when I watched your smiling face; when you were a little girl at your birthday parties, or at Christmas, when you opened your presents. I can't stand to remember your laughter or the sounds of your feet running through the house; or hearing your voice squeal "Daddy" any longer. I can no longer wake every day, searching the corners, in the closets of my memories, for precious moments to relive with you.

'And, I cannot be bitter about what happened anymore. I can't go on hating other little girls and asking myself why it didn't happen to them instead of you. And I can't go on blaming the ice. It wasn't the fault of the ice. I can't go on hating the ice cubes in my scotch. It was no one's fault, Amanda. It happened. I must accept it; and I must send your soul away from me. I can't go on living and thinking of your soul this way. I can't bring your life back. I can't. I must send your soul away from mine and stop pretending things should be different. I must send your soul to live forever beneath the surface of water. That's where your world is now, Amanda. You can play and laugh and smile there in the eternal vastness of the waters' deeps. Goodbye Amanda. My soul must leave yours now. It must follow what nature commands it to do.

'It must go to Marty's soul, and embrace it; and love it; and be one with it; and revel in debauchery with it. I can't help what is happening, Amanda. Her butterfly wing tattoo, and her lips and eyes, are vexing my mind, Amanda. I am losing those times when my mind returns to thoughts of you. I am so sorry; but I know I will think of you less and less; and of Marty, more and more. I know my thoughts now betray your memory; and they are so terribly immoral and wrong; but I am falling in love with her. She haunts my soul. Forgive me, Amanda; but I must go to her.' George's eyes looked at Marty. She noticed his tears.

"Now, Marty," Bertie became businesslike, *"I need to request a huge favor of you. Gwendolyn Lee, my closest friend, wanted to know if you'd let her join us on your next visit. She's very sweet and shy. She's gorgeous; but her husband and she haven't had sex in over a year. She was very quiet while watching your film. When it was over, she looked at me with her big doe eyes, and she started crying uncontrollably.*

"She wondered if there was something wrong with her. She asked me if she'd lost her attractiveness. I assured her that was not the case;

and that she was very beautiful. She put her head on my shoulder and said she didn't realize how badly she missed having sex, until she saw you. She said she was happy for you and remarked how lucky you are to have as much sex as you do.

"I feel terribly for her, Marty. She said she badly wants to feel loved again. She said watching you made her fall in love with you. She said she desperately wants to perform cunnilingus with you. Would you please permit her to do that?

"And, Marty, Gwen needs to be very discreet. She has a public following. She begged me to let her come to our next get together so she could meet you and be with you and get to know what it feels like to make love with you. She said she desperately needs to experience one night in her life when she can feel uninhibited and loved as a woman; enjoying sex again. You and she will absolutely love each other, Marty. I know you both will. Would that be, okay?"

"Of course, it will be okay, Bertie. I'd love to meet her." Marty nodded and smiled, assuring Bertie she was pleased to learn about Gwen. She was delighted that Bertie had pimped for her on a direct, person to person, level. Bertie was willingly completing her natural transformation from Amanda's mother to Marty's pimp, in addition to doing her dedicated work on Marty's film career.

"Oh, wonderful!" Bertie squealed and clapped her hands. *"I'll invite Gwen and make the introductions. I'm excited for both of you. We'll make it a girl's night! We'll have a WONDERFULLY YUMMY time.*

"Are you happy that I asked Gwen, Marty? Yes? She's shaking her head yes, George. Marty's happy, George! Our little girl is truly happy and beautiful, isn't she George? Her happiness beams from her gorgeous face in every scene. Your face telegraphs how much you love making love, Marty. It helps me pretend you're a beautiful virgin on your wedding night; making love for your very first time;

discovering how beautiful sex can be. That glow in your face comes through in every single scene.

"George, look at Marty's face in these next frames! She looks happy all through every single frame. Notice how happy she is, George. She's always enthused about making love with her partners. Her joy radiates from her face. I'm so happy for you, Marty, I could just cry.

"We must always pray for God to bless our sweet, innocent Marty, George. She's our precious, innocent angel. We're so glad you've found your happiness, Marty. We're all so happy for you. We all know you are doing what you love doing.

"Why are you looking sad, George? Oh, I'm sorry, George. I almost forgot about you. I'm sure it will be okay with Gwen. Marty, is it okay with you? George loves to join us girls and watch us play." Marty again nodded and smiled to Bertie. She was pleased that George would join in the fun.

"Good, then it's settled. George can join us for girls' night; and after we girls have finished, George, you can make love with Marty and help her have her final orgasm; and, you can make love with her, too, George. Let's not wait too long. Let's schedule our next session as soon as Marty has an opening in her calendar."

CHAPTER SEVEN

Never pray more; abandon all remorse; on horror's head horrors accumulate. (Shakespeare: Othello)

GEORGE'S SOUL

Bertie went downstairs to get milk and cookies for the three of them. She wasn't gone long; but when she returned to the bedroom, George and Marty were making love in the Missionary position. Bertie watched them a while before letting her presence be known. She listened to her own thoughts:

'My, she certainly didn't waste time for her first time; and, in my own bed no less. I've never stroked George's neck and French kissed him that way while we made love. She's teaching me something, I need to pay attention. What intimacy, what passion! They are beautiful together.

'Goodness, she's got him coming again; and, so soon after I had him in my mouth. Remarkable! Amazing! I never could writhe that way while also thrusting my pelvis into George's ejaculations. My God, she's the consummate love-making machine! I'll sit on this side chair until they finish. I'll close my eyes for a bit.

'Even with my eyes closed I can still see them making love. There's a sweet tenderness about it. It's so honest. She can't be an evil soul, sent to deceive me. No, that's not possible. Now, I can even imagine my own soul floating above the two of them; softly petting their hair, kissing their cheeks. Oh, goodness, I am blessing their love making.'

Bertie couldn't contain herself. She was smitten by Marty's shameless innocence and awestruck by her passionate lovemaking. Bertie got off her chair and knelt beside Marty. While Marty's arms and legs were wrapped around George; and while Marty's hands pulled George's buttocks down hard into her love cradle, Bertie stroked Marty's hair, kissed her cheeks and her neck, and massaged her vagina, under her clitoral hood, to stimulate her clitoris; helping her young charge relax and concentrate on her building orgasm. Bertie wished to demonstrate to Marty that she would do everything possible to fuel the nymph's eroticism; as if to prove her profound affection for her new love child. And as Bertie kissed Marty's cheek, her mind became made up. Her thoughts were certain now:

'I see that George has imagined himself to be his imaginary man who was watching Marty's film: LAY ROSES AT MY FEET. I see that My George has found his new love. He needed that. And I am happy for him. We have needed to make changes and it's time. And it's time to make another change.

'God, I am done with you, as in over you. You did what you did. You took my Amanda from me. Now, I am going to do what I am going to do. George and I will no longer go to your Church. We will no longer believe in your homilies. We will no longer pretend to be awed by your liturgical ceremonies and your priests' outrageously expensive trappings. We will no longer buy into your claptrap about all the reasons why your institution must be a sanctuary for pedophiles. We aren't buying your religious loophole arguments anymore. And, here's another pill for you to swallow. Amanda is going to cost you. That's right. You are going out of our wills. When we die, you will get nothing. Marty will get everything; our properties, our securities, our companies, all our personal possessions; everything. You heard me correctly. Why, you ask, are we doing this? Because a spirit butterfly told me to, that's why. When you wouldn't answer me, the butterfly did.

'So, we have changed our lives and taken your power over us away from you. We are willing to sacrifice everything we have, even our blood and our lives, to advance the fortunes of our new love child, Marty. Yes, she has become our new God and our new religion. We will worship her and pay homage to her, just as the ancient pagans did to their temple prostitutes. We believe in her now, not in you. We are becoming proud Pagans. We will be giving our love and our money where our love is returned. We will become ardent followers of Marty and encouraging others to do the same. So, you can stop sending your missives and calling us with your phone solicitations. Your priests are no longer welcome in our home. You have lost us. Goodbye.

'I know the choices I am making are for the best. I only hope George doesn't think I've abandoned him. He knows I'll always care about him. I know he will fall in love with her. That's only natural; and that's what I want for him. I want him to be happy. I only hope he doesn't fall so deeply into love with her that his soul escapes his control and he can't know his own mind. But George is a steady sort of man. He wouldn't let this consume him, would he? No, he wouldn't. Not my George.

'I feel noble, but weird somehow, watching the two of them while they fornicate; while I'm kissing her face and neck, encouraging her orgasm, supporting her lusting passion-fest with my husband.'

Marty began to orgasm. *"Yes, George. That's it! I'm starting to come. I want you to come with me, George. Let's make our first time special and beautiful. I want you to come inside me, George. Yes! I feel you now. I feel your hot cum flowing over my clitoris. You're beautiful, George. That was really beautiful. I love you for doing that with me. Hug me tightly and kiss me now. Yes. Oh yes!"*

"*Was that good for you?*" George whispered in Marty's ear.

"*Better than good, George. Honest. It was divine. Was it good for you?*"

"*The most wonderful, ever in my life. Honest. I've fallen in love with you. You knew I would, didn't you?*"

"*Yes, I knew. I wanted you to. I love you, too, George. We must make love often. I love fucking you. Promise me you will make love with me, many, many times.*" Marty cooed.

"*I promise.*" George whispered and kissed Marty's ear and cheek. Bertie reflected:

'*Well, that seems to make it official. Marty, my precious butterfly girl; my love child sent to me by the spirits, is our tribal goddess now; and it is her temple rite to take any man she pleases for her greater glory. This is precious and wonderful. I can see that they love each other. That is a blessing. And a blessing for George. They are making beautiful love. I need to become accustomed to seeing her with him; and her having sex with George in my bed, too, I suppose. I should feel guilty about my feelings, because I feel like I'm losing something, when I'm certain I'm gaining so much more. I'm gaining a daughter and a love child! How wonderful! I think I'm thinking correctly, aren't I? I mean, I'm not supposed to be inhibited or possessive with this New Modern Morality Standard, am I?*'

Later that night, after Marty had gone to her own room, Bertie slipped into bed with George. She didn't wake him for her good-night kiss. She settled onto her side facing away from him and stared at the wall. A tear formed. She was too lost in thoughts to wipe her face. It rolled down her cheek before she fell asleep. She knew she needed to accept what she'd done. She had set powerful, emotional forces into motion. She didn't know where they would take her; but she knew that nothing would ever be the same.

CHAPTER EIGHT

Good neighbors I have had and I have met with bad; and in trust I have found treason. (Queen Elizabeth the First: Her Majesty's speech to Parliament, 1586)

CONFIDING

Marty now returns her mind to the present and resumes speaking with David, looking into his wondering eyes as she speaks. David is amazed at her capacity for promiscuous debauchery. He is pleased beyond anything he expected or previously knew.

"Bertie frequently stops the film we are watching and talks about my work while she closely studies every frame, David. She always compliments my cock sucking and tells me she loves watching me perform fellatio, especially while my fingers hold the shaft as the penis's head exhales its cum onto my tongue; and while my fingers continue stroking the penis's shaft; and after the penis's head first erupts with its cum onto my tongue; and while I continue sucking out the penis's remaining semen; coaxing every last drop of it onto my welcoming tongue. She is absolutely spellbound fascinated by those scenes.

"George and Bertie both love seeing my eyes roll back while I'm having my orgasms. They have sex parties with other couples while watching my films. They all gather for this in their master bedroom. They claim they and their friends all get the urge to orgasm, while I orgasm on film. They tell me they and their couple friends even

orgasm simultaneously with me. They say they empathize with me so closely that they can feel the exact moment when I'm getting off. They say my facial emotions and my writhing pelvic motions come alive in their imaginations, like they're making love with me; and that helps them come. They sometimes watch my films for six hours non-stop at these couple parties. Bertie says watching film takes her mind away from the world's problems and political fighting. It's her new religion. It's worship for her. She watches my films for hours at a time, every single day.

"They freely admit they're addicted to my films. I'm convinced they are. They don't have any feelings of guilt about it, either. They swear they'll never go to another big screen movie theater unless it features me having uncensored sex. They claim regular movies leave them feeling empty and violated. They think the plots are bizzarro or stupid; and anything with violent content turns them off. But my films make them feel wholesome and happy to be alive. My films are all they watch now. It's scary to know that they obsess this way; but in all other respects they seem normal and well adjusted. They have watched other adult film stars, but now they fixate on my work.

"They remember my film scenes even better than I do; and they've bought every movie I've ever made. Often, after the three of us have watched one of my films, Bertie loves performing cunnilingus a second time by getting under me and resting my vagina over her face while I suck George. She's extraordinarily gentle and patient. She puts her heart and soul into the tender sensuous ways she kisses my vagina. Just by the way she works her tongue inside me I know Bertie deeply loves me; and she loves drinking my orgasmic juices. I'm convinced that her mind lives in my porn world's altered reality.

"They're both very sweet, kind, good-hearted, unselfish people. They always tell me how much they love my visits. But, there's something seriously emotional about them. There's always a Christmas

tree lit up in their foyer, year-round, with unopened presents under it, and one bedroom has a door that they always keep closed.

"They call their own bedroom their shrine room. It's a huge master bedroom with walls thirty feet by fifteen feet and a fifteen-foot-high ceiling. When George showed it to me that first time, I was overcome. My jaw dropped. On the wall behind their king bed is a gigantic thirty foot by ten-foot glass paneled picture frame. Bertie had it custom made for my still photos. It's her shrine to me. In her perfectly mounted photos, I appear to be jumping out of the frame into the eyes of the viewer. When I grasped the magnitude of Bertie's obsession, my mind began spinning. I was thrust into flashbacks of every film I ever made; every penis I ever fucked or sucked; every orgy, every threesome, every lesbian act, and masturbation. I was blown away; speechless.

"There are over a thousand five inch by seven-inch pictures of me seductively posed in various stages of undress; and photos of me sucking penises; being fucked with penises penetrating me in every imaginable position; in orgy scenes with penises thrusting in every orifice; with cum gushing over my nipples and breasts; with cum flowing from my vagina; with cum spurting from penises onto my tongue. At the center of this gigantic collage, she had over a hundred, eight by ten-inch gold framed photos. I examined them carefully.

"In every picture my lip gloss was perfect. My lips looked full and moistened, and very red and inviting. My hair was perfectly coiffed, or brushed out straight and flowing, showing its healthy glossy fullness as it played over my shoulders and down my back; or shining and glossy regal-looking where it was pulled up in a stunning chignon.

"My dark mascara and eye liner shades are perfect in every picture. My blush was a beautiful golden pink; and my eyebrows were shape-sculpted, and plucked to flawless perfection. My smile is enthusiastic and genuine in every single shot. Studying my photos

gave me profound respect for my make up and camera crews. I'm always prepped perfectly and filmed artistically. My crews accentuate my natural features and have me looking my appealing best.

"Her largest photos were extreme close ups. There were shots of penises shooting cum onto my tongue; of my lips burbling cum from a penis I'd just sucked; of my lips and mouth taking a penis into my mouth; of my lips kissing the head of a penis; and of my vagina in various positions and stages of copulating with penises. Some penises were just beginning to penetrate me; others were almost fully inside me, where all that was visible was the bottom inch of the penis's shaft; some penises were partially impaling me, and about half the penis's shaft was visible; some others showed penises that had just shot cum inside me, or had released cum onto my vagina's outer lips as they were withdrawing from me; and there were many other photos that showed cum oozing from my vagina or pooled inside me, and where my fingers were holding myself open, so film viewers could see the cum my vagina had drained from a penis.

"She also had twenty orgy scenes. I'm in different erotic positions with penises inside every orifice in many of them. In some I'm sucking a penis; and both my hands are holding the balls of my partners. My fingernails look perfect. I held back a laugh when I saw those because I know how Bertie is such a stickler for perfect fingernails.

"One orgy photo captured two penises in my vagina at the same time, with one in my mouth. It accentuated my red lips pursed lovingly on that penis's head; and it shows my face all aglow; and it captures my fingers holding the balls of two more penises, really showing off how integral my fingers are to making beautiful porn. And this same photo shows both my nipples peeking through rivulets of thick white cum, from the five cocks that had previously ejaculated onto my breasts. I remembered that orgy immediately. I was totally relaxed the entire time. It was one of my favorites.

"In other photos I'm smiling with anticipation as my fingers hold a penis that is about to enter my mouth; and I typically have my fingers holding another penis that's awaiting its turn to be sucked. Those photos also capture close-ups of my perfectly manicured nails. The best of these captures my fingers, with perfect nails, holding an extremely hard cock, waiting in anticipation. One photo practically screams how anxious a penis is to have time with my lips and tongue, while the head of another partner's penis has just begun penetrating my glistening open vagina. Every still shot Bertie selected illustrated one overriding theme: majesty. The beautiful majesty of sexual intercourse.

"I'm smiling in every photo. Bertie perfectly captured my expressions of pleasure. It's obvious how happy and thrilled I was while creating intimate artistry. She captured beams of joy radiating from my face in every single picture. Every photo validates how much I love what I do. You can tell I don't think of sex work as work. She also had about a dozen shots of me romantically French kissing my partners. They are hugging me with their arms around me; holding me tenderly, lovingly while I stood, partially undressed with my hand on my partner's penis; or while I'm posed, kissing my partner while I'm lying down in various stages of undress, or totally naked.

"The wall behind Bertie's writing desk had a matrix of over a hundred photos. These captured only my smiling face. When I first saw it, I assumed Bertie loved seeing my face in many poses; but then I took a closer look. Each photo captured a different facial expression that I had during different phases of love making. I had never thought about this, but a human face can express hundreds of different specific feelings while smiling. Bertie had captured many of mine.

"There were smiles of happy surprise, delight, thrill, amazement, conquest, ecstasy, satisfaction, anticipation, wonder, passion, *lust, joy, appreciation, amore, intimacy, and many more. Bertie had isolated each separate feeling that I was experiencing during different phases of love making in my films. Looking at my many smiling faces, I realized that images of my pleasure expressions lived in Bertie's head. Her mind became one with my mind through these photos. She internalized my feelings when I seduced and made love. She related to these photos and felt the same things I felt.*

"In this way, Bertie's mind became a mirror image of my own and her soul became one with mine. She wanted to capture and feel the same feelings a porn star felt while seducing and making love on set. But not just any porn star. Me. She wanted to emote my same surprise and pleasure at meeting my partner on set; my amazement surprise at how wonderful his penis appeared to me; my passion smiles during foreplay; my shameless, wanton pleasures, feeling him bonding to me and my pleasure, while his hand rubbed my vagina and he fingered me; the thrilling delight I felt when my partner forsakes all others and first penetrates me; my lust while we thrusted; my elation while my partner was perfectly pleasuring my clitoris; my astonished surprise smile when he pushed against my cervix, filling my love channel with his hard, swollen penis while we doggyed; my joy and amazement and elation when he ejaculated inside me; my intimacy and tender amore for him while he completed and withdrew; my pleasures with his love making while we kissed and caressed afterwards.

"She perfectly captured my 'come' smile. This is a special expression I give to my partner. I make it with my mouth open and my eyes pleading with desire. I give it after my partner has thrusted inside me, then slowed his thrusts, seeking to stay within me and not moving his cock for fear that he might ejaculate and end the scene. I accompany my smile with my words. I say: 'please come inside me. I want you to come inside me.' I nod my head enthusiastically when

I tell him this. I tell him I want him to shoot his hot cum all over my clitoris, and I want his penis to press hard against my clit while I thrust and orgasm with him. I tell him I want us to orgasm together because that makes intimacy so beautiful. Well, Bertie captured that smile.

"Also, she captured my smiles of revelry with my eyes rolled up while in the throes of orgy with seven handsome black men; and my scream of delirious joy smiles while their huge cocks were stretching my vagina. She perfectly captured my deep breathing: 'I can't believe how wonderful this is' smiles when I couldn't contain my pleasure sensations; and my frantic pleasure smiles which expressed how thrilled I was feeling for the long, intense ravaging I was getting, and wishing it would never end. She caught my marveled, grateful expression smiles while my vagina was being ravaged from behind, while at the same time my hands were eagerly stroking an enormous, hard black penis, and my lips were just about to begin kissing its gorgeous head; and yet another photo where my mouth was smiling broadly while opened widely, expressing my ecstasy and delirious sinful joy of wanton, unrestrained whoring; my lips were curled over my teeth, expressing my mindless nirvana; my tongue was fully extended and craving another penis's ejaculations; and my mouth was filled with semen while I was breathlessly receiving more ejaculations from six beautiful black penises. She caught that totally shameless whore smile at the optimal erotica moment. It was sensational. Bertie is amazing.

"While I sat at Bertie's desk and examined the photos closely, I noticed beneath each photo there were numbers, like 137, 28:39; or 68, 45:20. I didn't know what these numbers meant at first, until I thought about them and asked myself why Bertie was making numerical notations on photos of my smiling face. Then it occurred to me. Perfectionist Bertie had painstakingly catalogued my facial

expressions during each phase of love making in every single one of my 464 porn films. She was referring to my one hundred thirty seventh film, at the twenty eighth minute and thirty-nine second mark. That denoted the exact place in that film where my facial expression achieved optimal emotive perfection. She then selected that facial expression because it best captured the emotions I felt during that particular phase of intimacy. She created the still photos from the films. She notated these optimal expressions for her reference purposes.

"Now, while I am on set creating porn for one of my new, Bertie directed films, Bertie coaches me to recreate that exact same optimal facial expression she captured before, even if we need to perform the intimate scene several times to get my facial expression perfect. Bertie is a perfectionist. She's on a quest to create the most spectacular, spellbinding pornography ever filmed. She knows that creating the world's most famous porn star requires detailed study, coaching for perfection in all details, and an unwavering, uncompromising commitment to excellence. She guides my fans toward the same emotive bonding experience with me that she, herself, feels. She wants their souls bonded to mine; empathizing with me; feeling my tenderness, my passions, and my lusts. She strives to help condition my fans to unashamedly, openly, completely, and unconditionally, love and adore my explicit performances, and me. She is wholly dedicated to her task.

"Bertie spends countless hours, days, and nights, making certain that no detail in my make-up, my dress, my positioning, my seduction, and love making sequences, or my facial expressions are anything less than perfect. Bertie is better than facial recognition software. She coaches me to perfectly recreate the optimal erotic emotions and porn fan experiences. I value her dedication. I appreciate everything she does; and, David, I genuinely and honestly love

her. Her heart and soul are completely committed to enhancing me and my career. I adore her.

"Her photographs capture the genuine me. They illustrate that, above all else, I am a deeply passionate and unashamed lover of sexual intercourse with my many partners. Ultimately, my eyes were drawn to the center of her collage. A soft ceiling light highlighted the middle photo. It is a gigantic four foot by four foot close up of my vagina. I'm holding myself open with my fingers. Bertie took that photo herself, after she brought me to orgasm, using her portable electric vibrator.

"My butterfly tattoo and my bright red nails draw the viewer's eyes right into the center of the picture. I had recently masturbated. My vagina glistens from the oils Bertie used to prep me. My orgasmic fluids are flowing onto a white satin bed sheet. My vagina's coloration is spectacular. My creamy white surround mounds glisten, like they are crazed and thirsting for more lust. They beautifully, symmetrically border my pinkish red hued outer lips, and my outer petals perfectly border my robustly colored reddish-purple inner lips and my still darker channel.

"I was stunned when I first saw that photo. It froze me in time. I was taken back through everything every woman felt in the last five million years. I felt the yearnings of every single cell that made up my vagina. It wanted to procreate. It wanted to experience love, and give love. It wanted to show kindness and healing to the troubled world; and it wanted to feel all the sensations of human ecstasy when it copulated with a penis or a tongue. It was a living soul unto itself. It was a special, extraordinary silent omnipresent soul; unlike a human soul that can relate to people on their conscious level.

"It related to me on the same, deeper level that it relates to others, on their limbic level. It says to all human eyes that see it that it wants to come into their minds and reside within their minds,

forever. It wants the love it contains within itself to overwhelm, and displace, and consume all other thoughts that reside in every other cell in a human's brain. It silently commands all humans who see it to come into in and to let it reside inside their minds. It says:

'I am the female vagina. I am the beautiful origin of human creation. I make conception of life possible! I am here to love and be loved. There is nothing in the world or in yourself that is more important to you than I am. I am the One. I am the 'I am.' I am you when I am with you and I am you, in your mind, and in your blood when I am not with you. Love me. Honor me. Obey my desires, consort with me, conceive life with me, and I will bring you eternal joys. Disobey me, shun me, and you will suffer the miseries of my disappointment. Choose me over all your other Gods. Always choose me.'

"That picture of my very own vagina even turned me on! I stared at it for the longest time, trying to come to an understanding of how beautiful and compelling it was; and how it beckons a penis or a tongue to enter it. I finally understood Bertie's obsession on my own limbic level.

"I never fully appreciated the effect my vagina has on others until I studied that photo. I became transfixed while my thoughts wondered:

'What thoughts did Carl's wife have when she saw it? When she went flying off the mountain top, were her last thoughts, thoughts about my vagina? Did she think that my vagina was the reason she and Carl had no children? When her car tumbled end over end and crashed on the boulder field below, did she tumble to her death wishing she could have cunnilingus with me?

'When my murder victims are decapitated, what flashes through their minds as they realized their lives are ending? Did they think of their families, or did they lust after my vagina? Were they remembering how I displayed myself for them while I danced for them?

'When I stabbed that man and heard his moans between his screams, was his mind imagining the pleasures he believed my vagina would give him during those brief intervals, between my stabs? Did my orgy partners love kissing my vagina and fucking me more because they watched me commit those murders; or do they simply block out thoughts about my murders while they are making love with me? Did making love with me erase their thoughts of what I did, or did my murders increase their lust for me? Which intrigues them the most, I wondered? My vagina, or that I use it as my accomplice prop for my murders?

'And my lovers and Premium Members, do they see my vagina, as I am seeing it now; as a loving, giving, needing organism in and of itself; or do they simply see its butterfly wings and ignore how beautiful and inviting its lips and channel are? Can their imaginations know the heat my vagina often feels? I wish I understood the effect it has on other peoples' minds.'

"Well, David, for the first time in my life I appreciated the same yearning beauty that many others have recognized. The photo was a photogenic masterpiece, suitable for framing and sales. It's simply mouth watering and beautiful beyond words. It's the most wondrous, most sacred holy vessel of living creation art in the entire universe. I understood my own message. It's not just a snap shot of a vagina. No two are exactly the same. I could see I was especially blessed. Mine is exceptionally beautiful. Its picture comes alive. It gives silent voice to every woman's sexual needs. It figuratively speaks to the viewer."

Now, the voice of Miss Shameless resounded through Marty's mind, echoing her vagina's seductive, haunting message:

'Here I am! See me! I'm BEAUTIFUL and GLORIOUS beyond any words anyone could ever use to describe me! I am LOVE! I am LIFE! I am ETERNITY! I am nature's most holy creation! I recently enjoyed beautiful pleasures. Can you imagine what I've done? I ENJOY pleasure. I am insatiable for MORE

PLEASURE. Hear me. I am the insatiable voice of life. I want to MAKE LOVE. I want to enjoy pleasure, FOREVER; and keep living life forever.

'COME and FUCK ME. I'm holding open for you. I want MORE pleasure and I NEED more. I need MUCH more pleasure, so MUCH more. Do not fear me, nor shy away from me; never doubt my sincerity. I AM YOUR LOVING FRIEND; I'm HERE, holding open for you because I LOVE you.

'Surrender yourself, to ME; give your LIFE to me; give your LOVE to me. COME, TOUCH me, I want you to touch me. KISS me; yes, I want you to kiss me.

'Come INSIDE me; I want to feel you there. Enjoy me! Discover my wonders. LOVE me. I want you now. Come, my lust knows NO bounds OR shame.

'I want to gush ALL OVER your penis. I want to feel you coming inside me. My precious clitoris wants to orgasm with your penis inside me. I want you to feel my ecstasy and joy. My spirit will soar and twirl with yours.'

The longer Marty stared at the photo of her own sex, the more it beckoned to her and the more it hauntingly drew her closer.

'I'll love you until the end of eternity, you'll see. Yes, you will. You'll discover how wonderful we are together. Our lovemaking will be unforgettable and beautiful. It will lift your spirits; make you feel glad to be alive; and it will lift your hopes. The spirit that lives inside me will help you believe in yourself. We'll be wonderful together. You're going to ALWAYS want more of me, you'll see.

'It's time for US, now. I'm ANXIOUS to make love with you. I'M READY TO MAKE LOVE! HOLD me close to you. TOUCH me, FEEL me, and KISS Me. Hold me to your face. Hold your lips against mine. My clitoris is anxious for the loving touches of your tongue. Enter me. Lose yourself inside my lust. Become ONE with me. Come MAKE LOVE WITH ME! YES, YES, COME CLOSER. LET ME FEEL YOU NOW! OH YES! LOVE ME!'

"*That photo focused me like a laser, David. I understood, within the core of my being, what made my films the center of George and Bertie's universe. I wondered how many actresses have fans as devoted as those two. Also, I wondered about the world. Is it so corrupt, dishonest, evil, sinister, and violent that people are giving up on their traditional beliefs in government and religion? Are they turning more toward romance, sex, and intimate artistry venues to discover meaning in their lives? Might my romantic erotica help them heal their minds from the insanity of our world? Does it adequately convey my love for everyone? I hoped so.*

"*My film art is becoming main stream, David. People no longer feel they need to hide their sex magazines behind their classic novels on their bookshelves. They have the internet and social media now. They can watch love-making in the privacy of their device screen. They can share films with their friends; and invite them over to watch films in their home theaters. My films are the fastest growing purchases in the genre of intimate film art; and intimate film art is the world's fastest growing genre.*

"*Soon, my service assures me, producers will clamor for me to perform for the big screen; uncut; uncensored; and available for general adult viewing. The demand from the big theater chains is real and their distribution executives want me to be the featured actress because I'm already widely known for my porn films. They are confident that the prudes and religious types will be unable to prevent showings of my work. They believe efforts to censor my films will fail. They're betting that people viewing me making honest heartfelt love will help them find healthy reasons to believe in themselves. They've even told me that I'll make America great again.*

"*I wonder how they'd feel if they knew that murder is what I hold dearest in my heart. George and Bertie are so sweet and innocent,*

David. I feel this bond with them. I can't quite understand it. It's like a kind of love. It's not sexual, even though we do have frequent sex. It just feels different, that's all. I hope you'll never ask me to murder them.

"I once asked George about their perpetual Christmas tree, their collage of my photos and their closed bedroom door. He told me it's part of Bertie's grieving process. He said she'll likely grieve for the rest of her life, but that I'm a refreshing ray of hope for her. Other than that, he can't explain it. Bertie sees a shrink, but George says my visits make her happier than anything else. For years they let their sex drive fade, but no more!

"Bertie's now working on a collage for their bedroom ceiling. It will have hundreds of photos of my vagina with cum flowing out of me from different cocks. George told me that Bertie likes to lie on her bed and look up while she fingers herself, or while she makes love with him or one of her friend's husbands while imagining she is enjoying the same experiences I have.

"Eventually, George said, Bertie's goal is to have photos of me in intimate poses completely covering all four walls of their master bedroom. He said every time she looks at my photos one of them will suddenly arrest her attention; and she'll imagine she's in the scene with me, licking me and kissing my face while I make love; or massaging my shoulders and kissing my back while I'm sucking my partners' penises.

"George said she simply can't help herself, and he's totally okay with it. I've become Bertie's addiction. He said sex with me is the one thing that gives Bertie happiness; and all his life he's done everything he can to make her happy. He loves her very much. He said she identifies with me; adores me; and now that he's gotten to know me, he adores me too. He thinks of me as a friend and surrogate daughter. I've heard men obsess over film stars; but I never thought women did, until I met Bertie.

"According to George, her obsession grows stronger by the day. She maintains file cabinets in their basement filled with photos from my film frames and my still shoots. Everything is categorized in folders so she can examine a particular theme whenever the mood strikes her. She has, for example, a folder dedicated to my orgies with black men with their hands all over my body; another orgy folder with black men making love with me in every conceivable position; another orgy folder of me sucking penises of black men; and so on. She also has also a similar folder series of my orgies with white men, and another of me fucking and sucking men of mixed races. She has folders for every intimate theme imaginable!

"Some afternoons Bertie won't answer George. Then he goes to her basement file room. There she'll be, with the contents of a folder spread out on a table, staring at photos. She sometimes stares and cries uncontrollably. She'll get down on all fours and weep so hard she can't get back up. George told me he sometimes finds her on the basement floor in the fetal position, crying. Then he takes her up in his arms and carries her upstairs to bed."

CHAPTER NINE

*"The horror of that moment,' the King went on, 'I shall never forget!'
'You will, though,' the Queen replied, 'if you don't make a memorandum of it.' (Lewis Carroll: Through the Looking Glass)*

HORROR

After George understood that Bertie considered Marty part of her family, he finally revealed the events that led to Bertie's condition. George and Bertie were so enmeshed in their careers and outside interests that their intimacy had faded. Bertie confided to her best friend Gwen that George lost interest and he no longer had erections.

Gwen mentioned to Bertie that she and her other friends watched pornographic films. They swore the films helped their arousal. At Gwen's suggestion, George and Bertie started watching adult films. After a while they discovered Marty and watched her performances exclusively. They started watching her films for about a half hour every few days; but soon they watched her between one and three hours every day. Their home theater time no longer revolved around conventional films. They expanded their intimacy hour to the entire time from 8 or 9 PM until bedtime.

During their mental reorientation they recognized intimacy as a beautiful art form. George's interest in sex returned. He took erection pills for his libido. Some days he pursued Bertie. Before, when she sat before her vanity in her panties and bra,

George simply ignored her. Now he sometimes comes behind her, unsnaps her bra and initiates foreplay. He finger-teases her nipples and kisses her neck and back.

Before viewing erotic films, there was never a sign of life in George's terrycloth bathrobe. Now, it's often pushed eight inches outward by George's penis pole. Before, George had scant interest in hand stimulating Bertie or performing cunnilingus. Sex was about George getting in, getting out and getting off. Now, George behaves like a possessive bull. He often engages Bertie in hand play and oral sex. He sports his tent pole often and Bertie has amorous thoughts for the first time in years:

'My George has come back to me. My loins are alive again. I feel the same blood rushes I felt when I was a newlywed. George, you surprise me! I didn't know you still had it in you. You're a brute, George! You're the hero of my heart. Have your way with me, you stud muffin, you big guy! I'm waiting for you. Take me.'

Years before, George and Bertie had purchased new figure skates for Amanda, their sixteen-year-old daughter. She was home from Olympic figure skating camp in Colorado Springs. The new skates were perfectly hand crafted and fitted. They were exceptional competition skates. They laced tighter than her old pair, giving her ankles superior support. George had their precision high alloyed blades sharpened to perfection.

Bertie was excited to see Amanda perform her Olympic jumps on her new skates. Mother and daughter went to the same section of lake where Amanda had learned to skate as a little girl. The ice has no ripples there. It's smooth as glass. Bertie sat on a bench and watched her precious daughter race the wind. Amanda was about to make Mommy proud. She would perform difficult, back-to-back edge jumps.

Amanda was stunning. The young woman was radiant, proud, magnificent, and confident. First powering forward for speed, then skating backward to gather strength in her strong, graceful legs for her Triple Salchow jump, Amanda received Bertie's customary hurrahs and applause. Perfecto!!! Amanda's launch off her back inside edge; her knee bend; her arm extensions were all perfect. Her long, slender muscular legs glistened in the sunlight, her head perfectly centered above her spine, her breathing and her smile were perfect. Her landing on her back outside edge was graceful and firm; her knee bend was perfect. Everything about the jump was Olympic flawless.

Her new skates were performing perfectly. Now, racing forward from her Triple Salchow, accelerating for even more power, Amanda launched herself perfectly upward off her left outside edge, upward from the ice, going airborne like a bird. She leaped outward, lifting as if on the wings of a bird, gaining exceptional height; soaring skyward like a dove freed from gravity; displaying her perfect arm extensions; followed by her perfect pull in. With the sunlight dancing through her hair, she mesmerized her mother. She was the incredibly beautiful angel. She spun her body furiously like a whirlwind, twirling for the gods.

Amanda had challenged the impossibly difficult, Quadruple Axel. Visions of future Olympic glory flashed through Bertie's mind as her darling daughter sailed gracefully, effortlessly up, up, and higher; even higher still, skate blades flashing, dazzling hair, smiling face in the sunlight, twirling effortlessly through the air. She was now a splendid bird in flight; twirling free; breathtakingly beautiful. She did it! She did the impossible perfect Quadruple Axel!

Bertie knew what she had! It was there! She saw it! Visions of Olympic gold medals flashed through Bertie's mind. Amanda was one of only a handful of skaters who had ever performed the extraordinarily difficult, perfect Quadruple Axel. Now Bertie watched closely, her trained eyes riveted on Amanda's right skate.

Could her daughter finish it? Could Amanda, after her blurring spin, land perfectly on her right skate inside edge coming out of her four and a half rotations? Bertie clenched her hands, held them to her mouth and held her breath. Bertie sent her telepathic thought and prayer to Amanda:

'Yes, Amanda, you can do this! Yes, my baby, you will do it! I'm going to be the first person to see you do it!'

Then, horrors of horrors! Disaster struck! It couldn't be! It must be all a mistake! *"Noooo!"* Bertie screamed: *"Noooo!"*

Unbeknownst to Bertie or Amanda, the day before, a fisherman had cut a three-foot square hole in the foot and a half thick ice. The new freeze matched the old ice perfectly. The ice surface appeared as if the hole had never been cut. The thin layer of new ice revealed no hint that it was not a foot thick, but less than a quarter inch thick.

With all the might of her legs' downward extension force Amanda power slammed her right skate's landing edge jack hammer hard into the brittle shell of fresh ice. Her classic Olympian move was supposed to transition her gracefully out of her Quadruple Axel spin, and into her dazzling triumphant victory arc with her left leg fully extended, and held outward by her left hand; and that glorious display of her smiling, beaming, feminine glory was to be followed by her perfect spin into a pencil tight rotation with her thumb-hooked hands held high above her head. She would finish like a beautiful twirling bird, for her magnificent signature finish. It was the ultimate move that would separate her from all the other skaters. She would command the gold! The judges would have to give it to her.

But this time Amanda's skate didn't give her the reflex traction she needed. She could not make her breathtaking swan-like exit from her Quadruple Axel, with sunlight glinting off her high held left skate blade to wow her mother. Instead, horror of horrors! The ice shattered and gave way under Amanda's tremendous downward slam force. Circumstance, physics, and gravity conspired to doom Bertie's visions of Olympic gold, and Amanda's life. For one fateful split-second Amanda's beaming smile spotlighted Bertie's approving return smile. Amanda had performed that ultimate, nearly impossible feat, the magnificent, perfect Quadruple Axel! Her best ever! And, her last.

The next fateful split-second divided and telescoped into a thousand segments. Mother's and Daughter's eyes fixated upon each other's. They saw their life's dreams flash past them in review. The hours of Bertie's birth labor cascaded forward through the months of snuggling and bosom nursing; then further into the years when Mother ran after Daughter while Amanda learned to balance on her two wheeler; and then further still into her school years, her lessons and homework, her love of dancing and skating; and the endless hours of instructions and grueling practices; getting the best instructors, the best coaches; and the shooing away of pesky boys from Bertie's angel, this beautiful, budding Olympian sensation who could not afford time out from practice for boy-world distractions. The agony of Amanda's falls and ankle sprains and Bertie's presence to comfort, nurture and give Amanda courage to try again. All of those moments flashed before their eyes. Then, mother and daughter's eternal split second passed and was gone. Their eyes knew their dream world was over.

Both pairs of eyes realized the horror of the situation. Mother and daughter both intuitively understood that they were experiencing the death of their innocence. Their ordered, predictable world was coming to an end. There would be no Olympic Gold. There would be no more family attendance at religious services. Their God had turned his back on them. They were on their own; each of them cast into her new, uncertain, disordered world. Amanda, sweet darling daughter whom Bertie doted over and loved with every ounce of love that she had in her, was gripped by the hand of fate. She was wearing her death sentence. Her new, perfectly fitted performance skates were laced tightly to her feet through twenty eyelets. They weighed her down. Amanda would go into hypothermic shock from the icy water before she could partially untie the laces of even one skate. For that final fraction of their infinitely divisible shared second Bertie beheld and memorized Amanda's beautiful oval face, the high cheekbones, the Cupid shaped lips and the lustrous dark hair that defined her precious darling daughter.

In that glimpse of life before death, horrified Bertie knew they were celebrating Amanda's final act. Her cherub's face said all that could be said. It said:

'*Mother, behold thy daughter.*'

In that final second before her head plunged below the freezing surface Amanda's lovely innocent face thanked her mother for all the warm hugs and encouraging words. It said she would miss the secure home her mother and father had made for her. It said she was afraid, too. She knew she would never again feel the warmth and comfort of a good night's sleep in her own bed. The face said Amanda knew she was going away, leaving life, and surrendering her soul to the mysterious world of the spirits and the dead. The face said it knew it had to go and it wanted Bertie to remember it for how deeply it loved its mother.

But Amanda's body wasn't ready to go peacefully or willingly. She was a champion; the best. She had been trained to overcome adversity, to be a fierce competitor, a fighter who never quit. Amanda fought death hard. She fought because Bertie had taught her to fight fiercely and with determination through her sprained ankles and broken arms and bruises; but this was that one fight, that impossible to win, different kind of fight against her body's subjugation to the irrefutable laws of thermodynamics. Amanda knew she was fated to lose; but she fought regardless. She fought out of sheer terror and her refusal to quit. The icy trap pulled her down by her skates. Down, ever deeper into the freezing depths, plunged Amanda's legs; and then her body.

The numbing cold took the child's breath away. Despite this lack of oxygen her arms flailed wildly. Her fighting was fierce and furious. Her screams carried her anger message as clearly as her horror. She didn't want to die. She was determined not to surrender to the other world. She screamed the screams of the furious, the hopeless and the damned. Her beautiful arms flailed at the water and the ice walls with frantic determination. Water splashes rose above the hole and sparkled crystal-like in the sunlight, as if to mock the grace of the beautiful child being swallowed. But Amanda's struggle was no use. There was no partner to catch her fall, no surface to land on and break her wrist, and nothing to hold onto. If she could have sacrificed a leg break to stop her plunge into the icy water, she gladly would have made that trade.

But this was a different kind of fall, not a fall onto a cold hard surface, but a hard, powerful slam right through that surface into a freezing abyss. Her hands grasped first at one side of the trap's sheer ice walls then another, but there was nothing to hold onto. Try as she frantically might, she was unable to establish a grip on the slippery icy edges of the hole.

The icy water held her as if it had its own mind. The ice-cold water wanted her. It was determined to not give her up. It stole away her body's heat, and rapidly shoved her into shock. Her new, tightly laced skates were cursed foot weights now. They dragged her beautiful screaming face under the water to the bottom of the lake. Then those gleaming white tightly laced foot weights held her stuck there. She struggled to lift off from the bottom but gravity and her skate blades, captured in the lake-bottom's muck, bested her. Her beautiful highly trained body surrendered to its hypothermic shock, convulsed, and succumbed. Amanda finally knelt down and accepted her icy tomb.

Bertie screamed hysterically. She saw the final, frantic desperation in Amanda's terrified face. She heard her daughter's futile screams for help and the heartbreaking sickening gurgling sounds as her daughter's mouth opened below the water's surface. Bertie was horrified seeing Amanda's air bubbles. She knew the air in her baby's lungs was being replaced with lake water's freezing death. Bertie's screams were heard a mile away.

A man raced to help. He dove into the cursed hole to retrieve Amanda. He valiantly struggled to hold her head out of the water. But he was too late! An ambulance came. It also was too late! Everything and everybody came, but all were too late! Tragedy arrived first. The paramedic frantically pumped Amanda's chest and tried mouth to mouth resuscitation. The paramedic told hysterical Bertie he was terribly sorry, but despite everything he knew and did, despite everything his training taught him to do, his efforts failed. He told Bertie he could not save Amanda. Bertie's beautiful, precious, innocent Amanda was gone.

Days passed; then months passed. Every day of the following year Bertie went to the lake and sat on that same bench and stared at the very spot where she last saw Amanda's angelic smiling face, beaming with pride, as she looked that last time for her mother's affirmation. Bertie's mind asked God:

'Why?'

'Why was that ice patch cut away? Why did you let that happen? Why did you let Amanda skate onto that particular patch? Why can't we do this over? Why did you take her from me, God? How could you be so cruel? Didn't you know she was so young? Didn't you know she had so much life left to live? How could you take her? Didn't you know she was my whole world? Didn't you know she was the only child I had? How could you do this? How could you? Don't

you know how much I loved her? Can't you see how much this hurts? Tell me: HOW COULD YOU? Why won't you give her back to me? I want an answer.'

Then, she tried shaming God:

"You owe me an answer. Talk to me! Why won't you say something? Damn you, you son of a bitch, why? Please, please, please, dear God, give my baby back to me! I love her so much. I need her. Give her back to me. She was such a good girl. You had no right to take her. What's the matter with you? Are you proud of what you did to a lovely young woman? Did what you did to her make you feel big and powerful" Huh? You're no good, do you know that? Give her back! DAMN YOU, GIVE HER BACK! Just DO it! I'm angry with you. You shouldn't be allowed to do something like this to my beautiful child and get away with it."

Then, she tried reasoning with God:

"Why HER? She was a GOOD girl! What were you thinking? She tried her heart out to be the best. She was beautiful. She didn't deserve this. Do you find pleasure in what you've done to her? What made you decide to do this to Amanda? What? TELL ME! There has to be a reason. TELL ME!" Bertie sobbed hysterically, many times, asking God why, cursing God, and pleading with God.

"What do you gain by doing this? Tell me. I hurt so much; can't you see how badly I hurt? I hate you for what you've done. I guess that's okay with you, isn't it? Huh? Damn you!"

Then, she made demands of God:

"Give Amanda back to me! YOU JUST GIVE HER BACK! I want her back! I want her back now! GIVE HER TO ME! JUST DO IT!"

No one could dissuade Bertie from faithfully going to her bench, day after day and sitting there, staring at that spot in the lake. No one dared to tell Bertie she needed to let Amanda go. Staring, crying, and mumbling to herself while pleading with and berating and sometimes screaming at God, bereft Bertie's days lapsed into weeks, then months.

The distraught mother's life, dreams, hopes, and faith all disappeared into that icy hole on that cold December day. But Bertie thought, and prayed, and believed that perhaps, just possibly by the grace of God, her darling sweet beautiful Amanda would be returned to her. Maybe, she hoped, if she sat and stared at that spot where the hole was, and if she grieved and prayed and berated God long enough for Amanda's return, her daughter would come back to her.

Maybe she could make God feel ashamed of his decision. Maybe he'd reverse it and give Amanda back to her. Bertie hoped. Bertie was a woman of great spirituality and faith. She knew she could speak directly to God, one on one. She knew she could bitch at him, challenge him, and argue with him. But, most of all, she knew she needed to believe in him. But why believe anymore? What was the use of believing? That question, she could not answer. That was the what that she did not know.

CHAPTER TEN

I believe in ...., the redemption of all things by beauty everlasting, and the message of art that has made these hands blessed. (George Bernard Shaw: The Doctor's dilemma)

THE MESSENGER

Then, late one June afternoon, a Monarch butterfly alighted on the toe of Bertie's shoe. The beautiful creature looked at her and opened wide its wings, as if it was smiling to her. Bertie's spirits lifted for the first time in months. Her trance broke. No longer did she stare into the emptiness of the lake. Her eyes fixated their attention upon her delicate visitor. While she stared at her little companion a huge opaque ball of light descended over Bertie. She was visited by The Great Spirit of All Living Things. While immersed in the ball, she heard the voice of U, the Universal Spirit.

"Bertie, Bertie, hear me. Be at peace with your daughter's departure. She lives with me now; and she is happy. She knows love and warmth and goodness. You were a good mother to her; and you did nothing wrong. Her spirit lives within me and within all women who seek happiness. Look into the mirror I have placed before you. What do you see?"

Bertie turned her head and looked:

"I see a woman, a very beautiful woman. She is stands here beside me. She bears a close resemblance to my daughter, Amanda. I recognize her from her adult films that I watch with George." replied

Bertie, staring at the apparition of Marty, *"What does this mean, Spirit?"*

"I have my ways, Bertie, and I seek to bring happiness to people of goodness and faith, when I can be of help. Do not ask me to explain why I do what I do; only ask to know what it is that I have done."

"Yes, Spirit," spoke a contrite and hopeful Bertie.

"There once was a very special, lovely little girl who is now that woman you see. Her name is Marty. Her mother was not good to her, as you were to Amanda, Bertie. Marty's mother abandoned her, leaving her distraught for many years. She needed love. I took her woeful spirit into my bosom and gave her love. I have taken the spirit of Amanda into my bosom as well; and I have given her my special, eternal love. It is the love of life, Bertie. Now Amanda and I are giving that same special love to you.

"Amanda's spirit lives, Bertie, her spirit lives within the spirit and the soul of Marty, standing beside you in the mirror. Her spirit wants you to stop grieving for her and find happiness. The woman you see is a star of artistic intimate films. You and George have seen her films, Bertie. They inspire you and bring you and George relief from grieving. There are those who disparage Marty's film art, but Marty is a source of great joy to me. She has overcome great obstacles and prejudices in her life. She is one of my precious creations, as you and Amanda are; and I am proud of her. She brings happiness and hope to many who need inspiration in their lives during these uncertain times.

"Again, I say to you, Amanda's spirit lives, Bertie. She lives with me, even now as I speak with you. Amanda's spirit of freedom, and her joyful exhilaration also lives within Marty, as it does within me. Marty feels Amanda's exultations whenever she makes love. She knows Amanda's happiness and soaring freedom whenever she experiences the joys of sexual climax; when her frustrations leave

the earth and soar into the heavens; when her passions and desires are converted into sublime happiness and love.

"Marty, like Amanda, is one of my precious change agents. They are special because they show others what is possible. They encourage others to change and embrace life's beauty. They show others life's beauty in all its forms. I love Marty, as I love you and George; and as I love precious Amanda. You are all my creations. I love every one of you; and I am pleased with all of you. You are all good souls and none of you do anything wrong.

"I and my messenger must leave you, Bertie. I command you to go and find Marty and welcome her into your life; protect and provide for her needs, especially her need to be loved. Promote her happiness and well being. Instruct her. Teach her what it takes to become a top performer of intimate film artistry, her chosen field. Mould her into the best actress in her industry.

"And give her the greatest gift one human being can give to another, Bertie. Give her your gift of your unconditional love. Through the gift of your love, you will bring love and happiness into your own life. You have lived without inner happiness for too long. Your sadness must stop, and your joyful times must return. Join your love and good spirit with Marty's, Bertie. Discover peace and happiness in your own life, through her.

"You will know her by a butterfly tattoo on her upper thighs. Be with her and love her with the same loving sweetness that you loved Amanda. I have infused in Marty's spirit the same loving sweetness that she will reveal to you. Be close to her, Bertie. LOVE her as I command you to do. Be happy and accept that life is life; and life is beautiful. Life must always go on. Trust in me. I have my ways. Accept my ways. Never question them. Goodbye."

As suddenly as it appeared, the opaque white ball, its apparition of Marty and the voice of U disappeared. All that remained were Bertie, the butterfly, and a silence deeper and broader than

Bertie had ever experienced. Bertie watched the butterfly gracefully, effortlessly lift up as if its task was finished. It briefly fluttered before Bertie's face as if affirming everything U told her was true. Then, it fluttered away.

Bertie was shaken to the depths of her soul. She became transformed; suddenly freed from her worldly sorrow; freed from her cocoon of despair; and free to spread her own wings and flutter on to her new purpose in life. She left her lakeside sitting bench that day, never to return to it. Her heart lifted from its gloom like a butterfly lifting from chrysalis. A surge of warmth flowed through Bertie. Her spirit felt the warm glow of purpose. Hope replaced angst. Purpose surged in her breast again. She had work to do!

"George, darling, there's something I need to tell you." It was early morning. Bertie had laid awake thinking, as she had the previous seven nights after her visit from the butterfly. George was still asleep, but Bertie's decision couldn't wait any longer. She spooned George and began nibbling on his neck.

"Ummm, what are you doing, woman?" George was stirring awake now you. He rolled onto his back, and as he did so Bertie's fingers found his penis. She stroked him. Her kisses found his cheek.

"George, a week ago I was visited by a butterfly."

"A butterfly? Hmmm." George's mind was suspended between sleep and his wife talking about a butterfly. *"Hmmm, mum, what, you said you talk with butterflies now?"* George mumbled. He wasn't sure whether he was awake or still dreaming. Maybe he was experiencing a bit of both. He decided to listen.

"Yes, George, I was visited by a special butterfly. It came to me to deliver a message."

"Butterflies operate a messenger service now?"

"George, listen to me! This butterfly had a message. It gave me a new direction for my life. It gave me a purpose. I need to talk to you."

"Okay." George understood when Bertie got excited about something he needed to pay attention. Some butterfly had a message. *"What next?"* He mumbled a low growl, indicating he was ready to listen.

"I've been thinking, George."

"Mmmmmm." George sensed this could be serious and he dare not roll over and ignore her. Besides, her strokes and kisses were very pleasing. His eyes opened, fluttered a bit, and closed again; but he was awake now.

"George, you know that woman who makes those porn films we love to watch? That brunette with the red streak in her hair; and her butterfly tattoo?"

"Mmmmm. Yes, I know who you mean. What about her?"

"I'm going to cause changes, George, and she's going to help me. She doesn't know it yet, but she's going to become my project, my vehicle for changing things."

"Change what? Why do you need to change something?"

"I'm going to change the whole world, George, and I'm going to change her. I'm going to change the perceptions of the world she works in and lives in, for her and the thousands of women who work in her field; and for the hundreds of millions, actually for the billions of people who watch erotica."

"Whaaaat? What the hell kind of butterfly was this?"

"Hear me out, George. What that woman does on screen is beautiful. You've said so yourself. I've said so, too. What we have here is an entire industry that has been mischaracterized and panned as dirty and sleazy, as a place for women who are corrupted and have no morals; as if there's something wrong with them; as if society has the right to judge them, and snicker at them, while they're only trying to make a living.

"They are people, George. They are real, honest women who have to make a living. They may have no other way, but that doesn't mean

they are not skilled at what they do, George. They are performing artists, just like ice skaters, football players, painters, musicians, and opera singers. What they do with sex is artistic and beautiful, George. They are intimacy art performers, who work very hard at mastering intimate artistry.

"I'm going to rebrand their industry from 'porn' to 'intimate performance artistry,' George. I'm going to make the entire world see them the same way I do, as beautiful women performing breathtaking intimate artistry. I'm going to make the whole world love them and adore them and honor them and cherish their spectacular work, George.

"You know my determination and drive, George. When I set my mind to something, I get it done. I'm going to place intimate performance artistry on a pedestal, above all other art forms. I'll even raise it to a level of excellence, like Olympic sports. I'll even take my plans and programs to the International Olympic Committee, and get it introduced as a new sport; and I'll devise amateur programs that teach aspiring children how they can start participating as amateurs, with parental consent, and with proper age and practicing safeguards.

"That woman we love watching has a name, George. Her name is Marty. She's going to become our special project. By working with her to make her the best in her field I'll show the world how beautiful intimate performance artistry can be. I'm going to create in Marty the ultimate intimate performance artist. I will show the world all the fantastic things she can do during her love making. I'll work on her facial controls, body and orgasm expressions, and her vaginal control; and I'll showcase the beauty of all of it. I'll make the whole world see everything a woman really feels; and everything a woman can be, sexually.

"Marty will be the most audacious, shameless, guiltless, provocative, alluring bundle of breathtaking feminine sexuality the world

has ever known, George. She'll change the way men see women. She'll even change the way women see women. This is something that must be done, George."

"Why, because this butterfly told you to do it?" George frowned his skepticism.

"Yes, George. I absolutely believe everything this butterfly told me to do. And you are going to help me."

"You're serious?"

"Yes, George, I'm very serious. We're on a mission from some Great Spirit. Our mission will be like proving to the world that a young woman can do a perfect Salchow followed by a perfect Quadruple Axel. It will showcase sex position after sex position, Maiden, Missionary, and dozens more; methods of seduction after seduction, various love making techniques, and it will all be beautiful and flawless, perfect beyond description."

"You are going to change the world by changing the way the world looks at adult films and the women that perform in them?"

"Yes, George, I am! It's my purpose. Everyone needs a purpose for living, otherwise life has no reason. That butterfly told me my reason for living. My purpose will give Marty her purpose; and you a purpose, too. And, together, the three of us will give the entire world a purpose!"

Bertie's smile brimmed with confidence. She increased the pace of her stroking with George's cock to prepare George for a morning romp. *"I'm going to do this, George. And you are going to help me."*

"I am, how?"

"You have exactly what we'll need for many of our practice sessions, George. You have a penis!"

The thought of making love with Marty often and in many positions suddenly shot a renewed strength of life into George. His penis stiffened mightily in Bertie's hand. He was ready for sex now. Bertie rolled on top of him and began French kissing him. She glided his rock-hard cock past her outer lips into her eager, slippery warmth.

"See what I mean, George?" Bertie chuckled as she wiggled her hips on George's hardened joy stick. Her eyes smiled a ribald, mischievous smile. Her pelvis began a methodical, rhythmic grind on George's accommodating pole. *"I know you'll love our practice sessions."*

When Bertie set her mind to something she became an unstoppable force. She had a reason for living now. She knew it was not her place to doubt or question why the spirit chose her for this task. She believed she had experienced a divine intervention. She heard it command her to go forth; and to do what it had tasked her to do. She would work tirelessly to accomplish her mission. She launched herself enthusiastically into her quest.

She would first find Marty. She scanned dozens of web sites looking at adult film actresses, until she located her. Then, she purchased all of Marty's films and joined her Premium Member's Service. Before long, Bertie and George became mainstay clients of Marty's; and shortly after joining, their relationship with Marty became much deeper than a sexual one.

The relationship had a loving nature about it. It brought Bertie and George feelings of happiness they had not known in many months. Bertie took Marty under her wing. She convinced Marty that, if she was willing to work hard, she could become the world's foremost erotic film star. Once Marty agreed, Bertie assumed the role of her coach, the same role she had for Amanda. Just as she had committed herself to helping Amanda become the top contender for Olympic gold in the figure skating world, Bertie now poured all her love into helping Marty become the world's most famous adult film star. And, miracle of miracles, for the first time in over a year, Bertie and George made passionate love again, sometimes several times a day. Bertie's new direction was already paying dividends.

Bertie purchased a year's time from Marty's premium service; then set out to reshape her young project, as if she were raw clay. She enrolled Marty in classes to learn dancing, singing, acting; and figure skating to strengthen her leg muscles. Everywhere Marty went, Bertie came along. Sharp eyed and critical, Bertie corrected misunderstandings, miscues, mispronunciations, even errors by Marty's instructors. She drove Marty mercilessly until her charge had blisters on her feet from dancing, and pounding headaches from all the information her mind was absorbing.

The dancing, singing and acting classes made Marty into the most expressive, endearing, artistic woman in intimate performance art. Her expressions and delivery timings of her lines were masterful. Her vocalizations in certain scenes were opera soprano quality. Her body movements tantalized her fans. Figure skating gave her a special advantage over other competing actresses. Her legs were much stronger than the other actresses' legs. Her body fat got slimed down from a slightly chubby twenty percent to a tigress-lean, ten percent. Thanks to Bertie's relentless training regimen of exercise and diet, Marty became a sleek, muscular, feminine sex goddess.

"*Do I really have to do all this?*" Marty's feeble protests were more to slow Bertie's pace than to actually stop doing what she knew was good for her.

"*Yes, love, you do,*" was Bertie's stock reply. "*Champions are made, not born. You are a champion. Always tell yourself that you are a champion. You are the best in your chosen field. You need to have all these skills to prove you are a champion. Some adult film actresses just lie there like pieces of meat, getting pounded by a penis* while moaning and saying four letter words. They disgrace a beautiful, artistic genre.

"Others banter with their partners. They say a few provocative things before they lie down like a moaning piece of meat, mouthing four-letter words. They have little talent. Some will even bump their vaginas on a penis to the tempo and beat of the accompanying music. They are better, but not deserving of awards.

"But you, my dear, will act, and sing, and dance. You will set the standard for intimate performance artistry. You will tantalize and mesmerize. You will dazzle all who watch you. Men will lust after you.

"You will not even be an adult film star in the same way people thought of adult stars in the past. You will be a highly talented actress who also happens to perform sensational, intimate, erotic, visual screen art. You will be an artisan of love's most heartfelt intimate romantic expressions on screen.

"We will work with your writers to make your scenes realistic. You will dance in your scenes, speak dramatic lines with precision deliveries to the cameras; move and express yourself in finely tuned, finely timed ways. You will speak lines that reflect complex thoughts going through your mind while you copulate. Your fans will love and adore you for it.

"Sex happens in the mind. Remember that. Bertie will make men's minds obsess over you. You will go through a metamorphosis of sorts; from a skin flick performer to a sensational goddess of intimate artistry, much like a caterpillar transforms itself into a glorious butterfly. You will be intimacy's beautiful butterfly. You will rise to prominence, fluttering far above your competition. You will fly above them while they crawl beneath you.

"Other adult actresses will fall beholden to pimps and greedy agents. They will fall like butterflies into the oceans to be eaten by the fishes. But not you, Marty. You will be in charge of your own *fate. Millions of men and women lie in their beds at night, lonely for the hug or the touches of a loving partner. But in today's busy, disconnected world they never get that hug or that touch. When you are on set filming, think about those people as if you are that one special person in their life who gives them their hugs and touches and love.*

"That love will come through to the cameras because you will give your unconditional love to every single person of those lonely millions. Your state of mind will lift you above all other women in the intimacy genre. Remember: always give them the greatest romantic love they have ever known. That sets you apart. That gives you star power.

"No producer or director can own you. You are too talented for that. No one can tell you what you must do. You must agree to it. And it must feel right or you don't do it. Insist that your male partners treat you with utmost respect. Scream out to cut the film shoot if they don't. No man may abuse you. No man may pound your vagina like you're a lifeless piece of meat.

"Your producers must know and respect that you alone are empowered to decide who partners with you. If you dislike a partner for any reason, walk out of your filming sessions. Producers must understand that it's your vagina. You decide which partners are privileged to make love with you, not them. Every partner must have profound appreciation of your cock-savvy vagina.

"Every partner must express reverence for you. Every partner must exhibit passion and love for you; or you will insist that the scene be cut and that that performer be banned from working on the film. You will be the empowered centerpiece of all your films. You will be respected throughout the entire industry as its Goddess and reigning star. Producers and directors will be honored to work with you.

"*Your partners will cherish the opportunity to pair with you. They will know they are among the chosen few who may perform with you. Their appreciation will show in the films. The producers and camera crews will feel privileged to make your films. You will attract the finest production talent and best directors.*

"*You will be the world's undisputed number one star of intimate performing art films. And we'll promote you that way. Your time will command a huge premium over all other actresses. Your films will be premium priced. The exclusive aura we'll cultivate will earn crazy serious money. I will manage your Premium Service. Demand for your time will skyrocket. You'll see. Your rates will rise exponentially. You'll make more than you ever did. And you will work at a comfortable, sustainable pace.*

"*This hard work we are doing now will draw in others. Some will have marketing connections and they will want to promote you even further than I can take you by myself. But first things first. Today we head to the skating rink to practice, practice, and practice some more. You are going to torture your pelvic muscles until you feel like your legs are being ripped away from you while you are flying in mid-air. But you WILL perfect the Chinese Split. That will give you another edge over your competition. I have in mind a film that will feature the Chinese Split. When it is time, we'll shoot it. I believe it will be a sensation.*"

Under Bertie's torture regime Marty mastered leaping and spreading her legs in mid-air, while touching her toes; truly a remarkable feat. She used her newly perfected contortionist skills to perform a Chinese Split where her legs stretched away from her torso, revealing her vagina to the cameras as she settled herself upon a waiting penis.

While every adult film star could fornicate on camera, Marty learned to do so much more. She drove herself relentlessly. With

Bertie's coaching, she fine-tuned her acting, singing, dancing, and speaking skills. She learned to whisper her lines of erotic seduction while moving her body in ways that mesmerized her viewers. Stardom was in Marty's future. And Bertie knew it. She tirelessly molded her performing clay until she was pleased. She tracked Marty's progress with the passions of an Olympic coach and the ardor of a mother. She was ever watchful; ever critical; all the while becoming more pleased with her creation.

CHAPTER ELEVEN

In tragic life, God wills, no villain need be! Passions spin the plot. We are betrayed by what is false within. (George Meredith: Modern Love)

EXPOSING BERTIE

"There's more about Bertie's file photos, David," continued Marty. *"Bertie has standing purchase orders with three studios that create still photos from my films. When I make a new film; or when a studio learns that I've posed for a series of still photos; or that I've modeled a clothing line; or advertized a product, Bertie buys all those latest photos. She has the photos from every film and photo shoot I've ever done.*

"Whatever caused Bertie's obsession or keeps it going so strongly, I'll never understand. She's been like this for two years. Her obsession only grows stronger. She and George were deeply hurt. They tragically lost their daughter in a freak accident. Having sex with me; taking me into their lives, is their way of coping. It's especially therapeutic for Bertie. I don't understand it.

"After one of our orgasm games Bertie overheard me congratulating my clitoris on its championship performance. Shortly after that she asked me to move in with them. She insisted, saying I belonged with them, living close to them. She wanted to do good things for me to make my life happier.

"*She smothers me with motherly love. She told me I could have the entire west wing of their mansion with my own private entrance. I could have my lovers stay with me whenever I liked. She promised she'd never intrude on my privacy or do anything weird like that. She says she just wants me closer to her. Then she shocked me. She told me that someday everything she and George had would be mine. She told me they were worth over six hundred million dollars and they had no heirs or relatives.*

"*Bertie said she once heard song lyrics that said you should make one person happy and that would make the world a better place. She decided that would make her happy, too. She said she and George talked things over with their lawyer and decided that one person should be me. She told me she decided right then and there to commit her life to making me happy.*

"*I am not allowed to ask them why they decided to leave me everything, but Bertie said they were committed to their decision. She told me that she and George both changed their wills. Now everything they have, their six hundred million dollars, their homes overseas, their cattle ranches near Meeker, and their mansion would all be left to me. I couldn't believe what I was hearing, but now I believe them. Everything made sense once I understood the power of erotic romantic love.*

"*We started our relationship as casual sex friends; but things grew more intense and loving. I feel their love every day now; and I know they also feel my love for them. It's a deeper love than sexual love. It's more like a bond of trust and caring that we have with each other. Erotic film work can lead to that.*

"*A girl can just be out there, doing her films and private servicing work; when, unexpectedly, some wonderful people enter her life and discover that they honestly love her. Bertie and George saw my films and my performances as creating loving, beautiful happiness for themselves and many others who crave erotic romantic love. Many people search for romance, excitement, and eroticism. They hope to discover intimacy with someone. They want to give their heart to someone.*

"Bertie bakes a pie the day before I come. Then we always visit a while after we've had our sex. They ask me how I felt and what went through my mind while I acted in my recent intimate scenes, things like how I felt while I displayed my vagina filled with cum for the camera; or whether my smile and wink was just an act, or did I really feel that good about the session; and was I glad the session was finished, or did I really truly love it, and want to continue making love a while longer; or did my partner go soft on me?

"They're curious about all aspects of my life, David. They like to hear about what sorts of things I talk about with our Firm's salesmen while I'm squeezing their balls and stroking their cocks during foreplay; and about what things we talk about before and after I've had sex with them. They make suggestions that help me put more believability into my seductions, and more eroticism into my scenes. They give helpful hints about things I can do to get my male partners more enthused about love making.

"I started taking their suggestions. I now talk more freely with my partners about their penises. My banter goes straight to their limbic zones; and that translates into much better passion. Their penises seem to hear what I say about them, too. They definitely get harder and stay up longer when I praise them for how strong they are; how much they please me, those sorts of things."

Marty remembered her latest coaching lesson from Bertie:

"Your partner should be French kissing you at this moment in the scene; and he needs to be pulling your vagina tightly onto his penis at the same time; like his penis is lifting your vagina into the air; like you are flying into heaven upon it, freely by yourself,

above the world; soaring with supreme confidence in your sexuality. Instead, he's just hugging you about your waist like he's holding you down on the earth.

"You were having an orgasm there. It was spectacular, beautiful! Your face showed how much you loved it. You WERE in heaven. Your feet WERE off the ground. You WERE spinning, twirling with how much you loved how you were feeling. Tell your director to get that man back and REDO that scene. He needs to be showing how much happiness he has for you; and how thrilled and passionate HIS feelings are for YOUR feelings, while you are having your orgasm. Make them do that scene over again. Don't allow its release until they get that right.

"You did everything in those felatio frames perfectly. Your tongue plays upon and around the cock's head were sensational. Your mouthing of your partner's balls was just the right amount to stimulate your fans' imaginations. The way you opened your mouth and extended your tongue to receive his ejaculation was breathtaking. We'll use this segment as our base case benchmark. We'll compare how many downloads it gets with your future fellatio film downloads, okay?"

"Yes Bertie."

"Good. Now, I'd like you to try this in your next fellatio scene. It's an idea that should dramatically increase your downloads. Before your partner ejaculates into your mouth, I want you to stop filming. Take a day or even two days away from the set. Get some really good, deep sleep. I want you to look fresh as a morning daisy for this. Have your make up people moisturize your face with creams and moisturizing spray and get a full facial massage. Have them perfectly coif your hair so you look better than a girl on prom night; and put on freshened make up with a lot of mascara and bright red lipstick. Then go back to the set to resume filming your fellatio finale.

"Have some assistants get five penises, all readied to ejaculate. When the penises are all ready and primed to shoot, have two of your partners take their penises out of your helpers' mouths and insert them into your vagina. Then, I'd like you to fuck those two penises in quick succession, for a short while. Make them ejaculate quickly, gushing cum into you. After the second penis releases, quickly insert the third penis into your vagina. Have a fourth penis all primed to ejaculate into our mouth. At that precise moment, resume filming where you left off before. What the viewer should see is huge gushes of cum flowing out of your vagina over the shaft of the third penis which you are presently fucking, while that fourth penis is just about to come into your mouth.

"Before your fourth partner ejaculates into your mouth I want your vagina positioned on top of your third penis, while you face the camera. I want the camera capturing your smiling face and your vagina, with that third penis partly inside you. Then, I want the camera to do a close-in, full screen focus on your mouth. I want you to open your mouth at the precise moment that your fourth penis ejaculates onto your tongue. Now, this is extremely important. That fourth penis's head must be past your lips and slightly inside your open mouth when it shoots; and that cum shot must entirely release onto your tongue. None of it must get onto your beautiful face. Understand? Good. Then, after you have that fourth's penis's thick pasty cum inside your mouth, with all that white cum showing plainly on your tongue, I want the camera to do a real close-in focus, all the way into your open mouth.

"Then, I want the camera to stay up close, but back up a little to get some full-frame shots of your cum filled mouth and innocent face. We're going to make a vivid, explicit impression that viewers will never forget. I want you to seductively vibrate your tongue slowly from side to side, making the same motions a snake does with its tongue, while it tongue-scents the air; only you'll need to do those

motions much more slowly than a snake does them. We want your viewers to have time to fixate on the semen on your tongue; while you are giving them the sense that you are a totally, immoral, insatiable sexpot; who desperately wants even more penises to ejaculate onto your tongue. Got it?"

"Yes, Bertie, I understand the effect you want. You want me to appear never satisfied with the felatio I just gave and always wanting to do more, right?"

"Yes, that's exactly the insatiable effect that we're trying to communicate. You're trying to bond with all your male viewers by expressing how much you love their penises; that you are not concerned with what anyone thinks of your debauchery because your love of the male penis overwhelms all your inhibitions. You are boldly declaring that you are not an ordinary woman. You have no reticence about performing felatio, no hang ups over the immorality of it. You are fully committed to performing this particular sex act, because this is how you can best express your adoration of the male penis.

"Then, after you perform your snake tongue display, I want you to open your mouth widely and press your tongue tip against the inside of your bottom teeth. Slowly and seductively again move your tongue from side to side across the insides of your bottom teeth. While you do this it's important that you remember to smile with your face. Your cheeks need to be fully raised. Emphasize your smile of enjoyment. Your viewers will notice your subtle communication. They'll intuitively know your love of penises is genuine and not faked. I want every one of those men fantasizing that their cock's future will have a place inside your mouth. Okay? Got that?"

"Yes, Bertie, this is great coaching. I can do this."

"Good. Then, after five passes of your tongue over your bottom inside teeth I want you to close your mouth. Then, pop-blow five ultra seductive, slow inviting opening mouth kisses to the camera.

The effect we want is that you yearn for a viewing male fan to come to you and place his penis inside your mouth; because you are a craven, shameless woman, lusting to suck his penis. You are conveying that you have animal lust. You're craving to suck another penis and receive its cum. While blowing those kisses I want you to be thinking: "You simply must give me your penis to suck. Please, don't be shy. Bring your penis to me."

"I'm telling you what I want you to be thinking, because I believe what you think will be communicated through your facial muscles and your eyes. It's very subtle, but those telepathic communications do exist; so, we're going to make the most of them.

"Then, after you do exactly five mouth kisses, I want you to have a surprised delightful look on your face as you discover that, right next to your mouth, yet another, fifth penis, has appeared. Then open your mouth and move your mouth to that fifth penis as if you are just thrilled out of your mind and about to start sucking it. Then, smile at the camera and wink into the camera as you briefly lick the bottom of the penis's head, kiss its head; and place your lips gently, lovingly around that fifth penis. Then, I want the camera to fade out and end the film right there, with the fan seeing that fifth penis just beginning to ejaculate into your mouth. I want that viewing fan imagining that fifth penis is his; and you've just started sucking his semen out of him."

"But, Bertie, even I can't make a penis cum that quickly."

"Don't worry. We'll have an assistant giving it felatio, until it's primed to shoot before we place it next to you. When you place your lips on it and tickle its head with your tongue, it will begin ejaculating cum onto your tongue immediately, like it's on cue. I will manage these sorts of precision details. Got it?"

Marty nodded. Her eyes smiled at Bertie, letting her know that she wanted to perform the fellatio finale exactly the way Bertie visualized it.

"Okay, that's my beautiful, good girl. We're going to have you ranked at number one for a long time with that idea. It should make every red-blooded male fixate your image in his mind as the most shameless, unapologetic, sin loving whore that ever lived. Males' desire meters will read off their charts. Every man that sees this film will imagine his penis is that fifth one, that you've just begun to suck. Their limbic zones will become so overloaded they'll short circuit. Some of them will ejaculate from just watching you.

"You'll see. You'll become the idol goddess of the male world. I predict that scene will go viral. Downloads of the film will skyrocket. We'll charge $10.00 per download for it; and I expect we'll get a minimum of ten thousand purchases per day in the first month it's released. Even after it's been out a year, I believe it will continue making us ten thousand dollars a week for many years. Felatio, beautifully done, is better than owning a gold mine. Trust Bertie on this.

"Now let's study your next film. This is the one that smashed the industry's download records. You were terrific in your final erotic love scene; but I want to see you do that missionary scene even better in your next film. See where you're smiling as you orgasm? Yes, that's good, really beautiful; but you can make your orgasm routine even better. I want you to try this next time. You were already highly sensitized, right? Okay. You could orgasm any second, right?"

Marty nodded.

"Good, okay. You could feel your partner's thrusts, right?' Good. Okay, well, when you feel he's getting very close to ejaculation I want you to picture this in your mind. Your vagina is a heavenly channel and your uterus is the gateway into everlasting life. You are in the act of opening the gateway to eternal life, allowing your partner to enter.

"You are showing your viewers more than how beautiful you are when you orgasm. You are showing them the whole reason

why every human is alive; and that is for life to create more life. You are showing your fans that you are performing your divine duty. You are helping them see how glorious you are while you answer the spirits' sacred call to create life. This moment is much more important than anything else your fans could ever see. It's more important than a football game or an orchestra concert or a Broadway play; and you must convey how splendid this creation by conception moment is.

"So, just before your partner releases, I want you to undulate *your stomach muscles in rhythm with your pelvis, as smoothly as you possibly can. I'll have your cameraman zoom in very closely on that motion, because it sends a message. It says that you are opening the gates of life to him, beckoning him to enter into your holy of holies and create a sacred union with you. I want your mind thinking that you are opening your gates for him, okay? You want to appear to the camera that you are an insatiable, tireless love-making goddess. Your message is that you will open your gates for all who seek the beauty of eternal life. inside you. Got it?"*

Marty nodded again. Her eyes told Bertie she was paying close attention.

"Good. Then, while your partner is shooting his semen into you, *I want you to do more than just lie there and beam your happiness. I want you to beam your beautiful happiness face into your partner's eyes; and have the cameras do a close up focus on your face to capture that. Then, I want to see your hips and pelvis lifting up, pushing your vagina hard up against his cock, taking all of him inside you. Okay?"*

Again, Marty nodded with the serious look of a student learning from a wise teacher.

"Very good, then I want to see you roll slightly from side to side *as you wrap your legs tightly around his waist and pull his body down hard into you. The effect I want to see is that you savor the act of taking his semen inside you; and that you are determined to take every last drop of it away from him.*

"While you are doing this, I want you to be thinking that you are pushing his cock through the door of life and taking all of his life into your life to make new life; and I want your legs to reflect that you are closing the doors of life, behind his cock; capturing his sex inside you, keeping his life forever inside your holy place of life; holding it fast to you while preventing any of his life from leaving you. All this, while you are taking from him, all the life he has to give you and commit to you; and keeping it forever inside your life. Okay?"

Another head nod from Marty. Her eyes told Bertie she respected her flair for coaching.

"Good, wonderful; and, finally, I want you to reach up to your partner's face with your hands and hold his face and look into it with that look of awestruck, heavenly love that you do so well; and then pull his face down to your face and smile your loving smile to his face while you continue your semen capturing rocking motion. I'll have the cameras play back and forth, between your two faces; to capture the look of adoring, commitment love between the two of you, while you roll softly back and forth with his cock inside you. I want to see your copulation motion combined with feelings of love, Okay?"

"Yes, oh definitely yes, Bertie, I'm visualizing this. I can't wait to perform it on set."

"Very good, that's my girl. Then, French kiss with him, like you love him as though he's your god; and he's just blessed you with his creation seeds. Got all of it now?"

"Oh, yes Bertie. I'm really anxious to show you I can do the scene this way, exactly the way you want it done."

"Good baby, let's run through that exact sequence next time. You'll see that our viewer downloads will go even higher than they do for the film with the felatio scene.

"And there's one more thing I want to have you change at the end of every performance. I notice when your partner is finished you display your vagina to the camera. You show your vagina cum pool and smile. From now on I want you to first look into the eyes of your partner, and then smile your most satisfied, enthusiastic smile; and then I want you to make lip kisses; then send those lip kisses to him, like you can't wait for him to come back to you and make erotic love with you all over again, because it was that wonderful. Think of him, no matter which partner he is, as the greatest lover you've ever known.

"After you do those kiss-sends to your partner, rotate your hips to the camera and display your opened vagina and your triumphant cum pool. Yes, every single time. Hold yourself open with your hands so your viewers can see your inner lips. At that point I want to see you make three lip kiss-sends to the camera, as if the camera is your next lover; and you want it to come to you and make wild passionate love with you. While you do this, I want you to flex your buttocks slowly for each of your kiss sends and imagine that your vagina is an opening rose bud.

"Push yourself closed with your hands so the viewer can see the white cum pool rise to float on the surface of your vagina; and then open yourself again, so the white pool disappears again, inside you. Your audacious wanton messaging's implication is that you are beckoning more penises to come to you and deposit more cum inside you. It will be sensational catnip for male viewers. It will stay in their minds. They will think about you, and dream about you, long after they see your films. It will become your signature sign off message.

"Be thinking that you are opening yourself for your viewers to come to your beautiful rose and adore it; enter and make passionate love with it, they will be eager to lose their cares inside you. Make them feel that you are anxious for them to release their cares inside you. Think. You are signaling that you want them to come to *you and surrender their semen inside you. Convince them that you want to make love with them. Offer yourself as their mind's ultimate escape from reality. Remember that. Are you agreeing with me, George?"* George had stopped paying attention several minutes before. He imagined his face was buried in Marty's vagina, performing cunnilingus with the fascinating nymph. That took away his focus.

CHAPTER TWELVE

Frustrated, feeling controlled, manipulated, lied to, trapped, over-worked, under appreciated, helpless, desperate to change things? Do something about it! (Rosemary Ness-Bitner, author)

DEMANDS

"There's a reason I want you to perform this "come hither" routine as your signature sign off at the end of your films." Bertie explained the mental state of many humans in the modern digital society. Marty was paying attention; George, not so much.

"People are stressed. Their worlds have gone to hell. Advertizing, constant interruptions, political bickering, and corruption are rampant. Family tensions, strained friendships, deadlines, and tight schedules squeeze people hard. The wealth effect sucked the life out of America's middle class. It's gone. Only the lower and upper classes remain. The lower-class crawl like feral animals. The wealthy take private jets.

"But the wealthy are neurotic. They sense a revolution is brewing. They fear it because they know they caused it, but they don't understand how. Murders, suicides, and rapes indicate something ominous comes. Everyone wants to escape it; but to where, back to Mother's womb? No, that's too tricky. But to where, then?

"How about a place where no one knows hurt or stress, where all is bliss, and where everyone knows your name? Once upon a

time, the movies were that place. No more. Violence, poor acting, mind numbing special effect explosions, and nonsensical plots have killed the escape factor; so, too, have disease phobias. How can one escape? What's left? How about losing oneself in innocence and love?

"Marty, viewers see innocence and love in your face. They want to escape into it, and into you. They succumb to your beauty. They fall in love with you. They fantasize exchanging the life they have for a new life with you. It's natural.

"So, Marty, when viewers see your open, welcoming vagina, they receive a powerful subconscious message. It tells them you will welcome their life's seeds. They think they can escape; go back in time; rediscover the bliss they knew as fetuses in Mothers' wombs. Their subconscious recreates their lives. And in these fantasies, they make love with you, from their lives' inceptions. They imagine they are a valiant sperm seed, swimming from your semen pool, merrily through your cervix, up through your fallopian tube into your womb where they will meet an egg from your ovary. There they will repose in eternal happiness.

"They receive a subconscious vision. Sanctity, creation through conception's lust-love and reincarnated life are, in their minds, theirs for the taking. Their needs are met. Through you, they discover escape. They leave their dreadful stressed-out lives and enter their new lives. They find true love and happiness.

"They associate their perfect, imaginary lives with your films. And that results in download sales. Your viewers must believe that you LOVE loving them. That's why they watch you. They are not receiving that love in the lives they are living; so, instead of thinking that they are paying to watch you screw; they believe that they are paying to receive hope for a new life.

"Hold that thought while you open your vagina and mouth your lip kisses to that camera. Imagine you are offering your fans the pathway to eternal happiness. Their eyes will read your thoughts

in your face. Their minds will hold that image in their hearts; and they will keep them in their dreams, forever. It will mean everything in the world to them. It will make them adore you. Trust Bertie on this. Your paying downloads will skyrocket, and your fan base will explode. You'll separate from your competition. You'll gain more fans than the next ten adult film stars combined.

"Remember, you are the world's gold standard of sex. It's all in your attitude. Do not settle for silver or bronze. We want your fans thinking your orgasms are the greatest outpouring of love and ecstasy they've ever seen. Always believe your orgasms are the greatest, most spectacular Olympian moments of ecstasy, ever! You create films because you love sex; but remember, you are also on film to demonstrate to your fans just how wonderful and spiritual love making is.

"Your fans' viewing pleasure will be most effective when you imagine there's a fan out there anxious to come to you. Be thinking that you want him to come to you; and he wants to give you all the love he has.

"Let your feelings of love and lust, your wild delirious joy, your welcoming pathways to eternal life, express themselves. Share those imaginary experiences that your audiences crave. Be their portal to their new universe, where all is blissful and loving.

"Think those thoughts. Telepathically enter the minds of your fans. Help them imagine that you are their pathway to rebirth, that through loving and adoring you they will become like semen in a mating butterfly. They'll entrust their fantasies to you. They'll imagine that their new glorious lives will rebirth within your vagina.

"There are special, mouth-watering empathetic moments in your films. Those moments create that difference between your top ranking and all those lesser stars who follow. Remember, you stand alone and apart. You are Queen of Intimate Art! No one shares the gold platform with you. Always remember, it is all about your attitude! Your thoughts and attitude make the difference.

"You will be the foremost box office sensation in big screen the-aters. People, especially men, are tired of watching female actresses splatter their emotions across the screen. They are tired of seeing women scream hysterically at their male counterparts. They are exhausted with women who stomp their feet; throw their clothes around like mindless twits; act their faux acts of exhausted, hurt, ignored, ashamed, embarrassed, frightened, giddy crazy happy, and other emotive blasts that film screen writers put them through. It's overdone and stupid.

"Audiences are ready for a woman who does what women were put on earth to do; make love. People will prefer paying to see a woman hold her man in her arms, kiss him and make love with him over paying to watch a woman have an emotive binge-out. People do not want their emotions tossed into a blender. It's exhausting. But making love can never be overdone. That's where you shine, Marty. You will shine and twinkle like the star you are!'

CHAPTER THIRTEEN

Can love be controlled by advice? (John Gay: The Beggar's Opera)

ADVICE

"David," Marty resumed explaining her relationship with George and Bertie. *"Sometimes I feel like I'm Bertie's daughter. She asks me how my work week went. She always gives me her encouragement and emotional support. I can feel her love, even when I'm not with her."*

It was during one of Bertie's question and comment sessions that Marty's voices chimed in with their own thoughts about her career. Misses' Promiscuity, Shameless, and Iniquity all spoke to Marty in unison:

'Look what has happened girl! You've become famous. Bertie isn't the only one obsessing over you. You have millions of fans now. Your film sales are skyrocketing and your appointment service is going crazy. Your service says you must raise your prices. There is overwhelming demand for your private sessions. You can't possibly fuck all these men who are calling for you. So, raise your prices. Charge ten thousand dollars for a one-hour private session instead of five thousand. Charge fifty thousand for a film of a half hour and a hundred thousand for a full hour. You are no longer competing with street girls, and whores working out of massage parlors, chat rooms and cocktail lounges.

'Look where you are! Look how far you've come in just two short years of making adult films. You have fucked, sucked, and licked your way to the very top of whoredom. You are a marketable brand. You are the most sought-after intimacy actress ever! You are THE most desired woman in the entire world! You have opened America to The New Modern Morality Standard. You've shattered stereotypes. You've made intimacy a cause célèbre and reshaped America's morals.

'You've removed the stigma from prostitution and erotic art. You've redefined normal, everyday behaviors to include prostitution and eroticism; and you've glorified it! Even better, you've deified it! You've changed the film industry! Corruption sagas, spook thrillers, idiots chasing other like idiots with guns drawn; buildings blowing up; people being punched and stabbed, are all passé. This is YOUR time. YOUR brand has caught fire. Shameless, uninhibited, beautiful explicit, erotic sex is what the people crave now; and YOU are the world's top ticket.

'When you walk into the Intimacy Performance Artist Awards Ceremony your fans will be lined up twenty deep to see you. When they get a glimpse of you, they will scream uncontrollably. Many women will faint. Many men will rush the security lines just so they can touch your dress. You may encounter crowd madness. Your dress represents a trophy to some. They see it as a shroud that covers the hottest, most beautiful, wonderful, delicious, fuck-loving vagina of the world's most desirable goddess. Expect attempts to kiss your smiling, winsome face, and your delicious lips; even to rip your clothes from you. Your fans are delirious over you. You are above and beyond red hot to them. They may get out of control. Be ready for anything.'

'Marty,' Miss Promiscuity spoke alone. 'I don't know how today's visit with David will work out. I kind of thought he'd want sex with you, but now I don't know what to think. Please don't be upset with me if he sends you away without even touching you. He's weird. But, try not to think about him. Look at all the good things that have happened for you because you followed my advice.

'Remember when Donny and Billy drove you and Maria to Ocean City? Remember when Donny first put his hand on your vagina and I told you that that was a good and beautiful thing; and that you should leave his hand there? Do you remember how you felt? Remember how grateful you felt that I gave you that advice? Remember how you felt connected to Donny; how you felt like you and he belonged together; how you felt complete trust in him; and how you suddenly realized that you were like a goddess to Donny? You rode in that car with your right foot propped out the window, your head relaxed on Donny's big shoulder, your skirt way up above your knees, and Donny's hand massaging your vagina through your panties, remember? You felt good about yourself, about Donny and your sexuality; and about your self-esteem, everything; remember?'

'Yes,' thought Marty. 'I remember.'

'That's the result of following my good advice, Marty. That advice led to Donny and Billy fucking you, which led to all your dating; and then to prostitution; your romances with Darren; the Four J's; and then to your position at U G G A; to Bob and Carl, and your fabulous film career; and now to Bertie and Gwendolyn. I've given you the correct advice all your life. Basically, I've told you that if you feel like making love with someone, you should always just do it, and never feel guilty about it. But, Marty, this obsession you have with David doesn't feel the same to me as your other loves. I think you should listen to Miss Iniquity about him. Something doesn't feel right about him.

'Look where we are, Marty. Do we really need David? Really? Bertie introduced you to her dearest friend, Gwen, a multi-billion-airess. Just a week after you and Gwen first had cunnilingus together, she fell in love with you. She gave you that beautiful jade neckless.

She placed a permanent twenty-five-million-dollar credit line with your appointment service; paid your membership to her exclusive private jet service company; bought you multi-million-dollar apartments in New York, Washington, London and Paris, her favorite cities. That woman is a true friend. She asks nothing in return for her gifts. She's not like David. Sure, she invites you to join her on her yacht in Monte Carlo; and on her art buying junkets to her favorite cities; but she only does that as your true friend. She's not like David. She makes no demands on you.'

CHAPTER FOURTEEN

Lesbia hath a beaming eye, but no one knows for whom it beameth.
(Thomas Moore: Lesbia Hath)

GWEN

Marty's thoughts interrupted Miss Promiscuity's ramblings, taking her back to her most recent weekend with Gwendolyn and the things Gwen was saying:

"*You know I've fallen in love with you, Marty. There's nothing I wouldn't do for you. I want you to know that.*" Gwen was grinning from ear to ear as if she was a young girl again, frolicking on the lawn with Max, her French Poodle puppy.

"*I want you to have this diamond and ruby choker neckless with matching earrings, foot, and arm bracelets. I'd love it if you'd please wear them one time when we make love because; well, Marty, I don't know any other way to express myself. Your love and our friendship are priceless to me. So, please, won't you accept these and wear them for me, just one time, pretty please?*"

"*Of course, I will, Gwen; but, honestly, Gwen, you're being way too generous with me. I mean the houses and the cars and the furs. I never expected those things from you. And then just last week you gave me a hundred-thousand-dollar gift card to Adam and Eve, the adult toy store. You don't have to overdo things like this, Gwen. Don't get me wrong, I love your attentions and I love you, too; but how many vibrators and sets of sexy lingerie do you think I need in a year?*

"I love wearing their exotic nightgowns and panties for you, and I love the way you like to feel me under my panties; and you know how I get so blistering hot for your tongue when you start peeling my panties down my legs. Oh, Gwen, I just feel there's something I must do to please you more, to help you know how much I love you, too. I truly love you, Gwen.

"Right this very moment I want you next to me naked in our bed. I want to touch you everywhere and watch you smile and laugh while I part your thighs and kiss them, going higher and higher until I'm finally home where I belong. Help me, Gwen. Take me to happiness with you. Take me to that wonderful world that only you and I can understand. I need to kiss your lips, your vagina; and I must kiss your clitoris. Oh, Gwen, please, let's not go out tonight. I don't want dinner. I only want you, just you."

Marty remembered how she and Gwen made long, passionate love their first night; how Gwen was passive at first, letting Marty's tongue find her sex; and tenderly stroking her clit until Gwen's first, massive eruption. Success! It was exactly what Gwen needed. For all her money, love and affection were the intangibles that Gwen needed most. Gwen believed that a good evening with Marty was priceless.

Gwen did not particularly care for men. She thought them brutish, self centered, void of true emotions, short sighted, smelly, careless, rude, inconsiderate, and thoughtless. As her beautiful companion and sincere honest lover, Gwen valued Marty deeply. Gwen's ability to share her life's experiences was the succor of her life. She could never give away more money in a year than she took in. She was in a rarified class of women, the uppermost wealthy of her gender; free of any male's control.

Marty daydreamed of the many times Gwen cradled her, kissed her mouth while circling a vibrator over her vagina before she grappled her thighs and engaged their sixty-nine positions. It was Gwen's preference for their love making. It was beautiful; fulfilling uninhibited bonding.

Despite Gwen's love of cunnilingus and her facility with dildos, Marty found herself wishing she could have Gwen's same endearing qualities in a man. Bob met all her requirements for closeness, but closeness alone could not displace her erotic cravings for Carl, Josh, Marshawn, and some others.

Meanwhile, Miss Promiscuity would not give up. She was adamant that Marty ditch David and concentrate on her relationships with Bertie, Gwen; her male partners and lovers; and her film career. She continued singing Gwen's praises:

'She doesn't make you stay in her homes. She always gives you your choice to stay in your own home and she always respects your choice. She always pays your service double rates for those days when you travel with her, so your service can rearrange your appointments. When she wants to have you arrange a private orgy party for her, she always pays your male performer friends double their usual rates; and she pays their travel and hotel costs in the cities you visit. That's how considerate she is!

'Gwen is a classy lady, Marty. She LOVES you. She values your privacy. She NEVER asks questions about what you do with your male performers the night before or the day after her orgy sessions. She bought you those homes because she intuitively knew that you'd often want to spend your nights with your male friends.

'She's empathetic. She ALWAYS thinks about YOUR happiness. She understands about your sex addiction and your need to fuck. She totally gets your nymphomania. She respects that deeply personal need. So, Marty, I think it's time we do more with your

Premium Service and Gwen, and Bertie's film efforts; and less with David. Think about that. I've got to side with Miss Iniquity on this one. She is very skeptical of David.'

'*I know you're making a lot of sense, Promiscuity,' Marty replied with thoughts of her own. 'But there's one thing that David understands about me that no one else does, not even you, my voices. Many people believe that whores are heartless. They think whoring is just about the tricks and the money. Well, for the Johns, or tricks, that's sort of true. But then there's this paradox that contradicts everything people think they know about prostitutes. We are people who have needs, especially our real need to be loved. Well, my close lovers, especially Bob and Carl, fill that real need. And, David fills another, even deeper, need. He's my connection to my family need, Father. Father was the only family I ever had.*

'*I couldn't live if I didn't have ways to fulfill my needs. I couldn't live without Bob, Marshawn, Josh, Carl, and David. So, I pay a price to fill those needs. It's what I must pay to continue being who I am. Every whore pays a price. For every woman that succeeds in adult films, twenty wash out. Some end up druggies; some alcoholics; some get beaten and busted up; some get their spirit broken; some even get killed. Why do they let themselves get abused so badly? Because once they start doing adult films they can't go back to normal, whatever normal is. They get into this cycle of needs and fulfillment of needs. Prostitution becomes the way to get those needs fulfilled. Some do tricks to earn the love of their pimps.*

'*I do film and private service because that gets me the adoration, love, and sex I need. The love I get from Bob and Carl and my others is not enough to satisfy my nymphomania. I also need to spread the gospel of the New Modern Morality Standard. That gets me my shrink's, Mrs. O'Dell's, approval, which I also need.*

'*I do the murders because they give me David's approval. That provides me with my career platform, my front, my appearances of a legitimate career. And performing my murders gives me spiritual access to my father. That's why murder fulfills my greatest need. It gets me closer to family. These are my choices, Promiscuity. So, you understand, don't you; everything I do is perfectly logical? This is my career. It's not a career for Scaredy Cat pussies.*

'So, don't be so hard on David, Miss Promiscuity. Stop trying to drive a wedge between me and David. If things go wrong with me and David, it will be your fault. And Miss Iniquity's fault, too. Don't make me lock the two of you in my mental closet. I need your advice for so many things. But stop trying to give me advice that you know I can't follow. Remember, you and Miss Iniquity understand one part of me. But David understands me in a completely different way. And that is my secret way, okay?

'David understands my hot button. He knows I'll pay his price to satisfy it. He knows every time we murder someone, I experience my special emotional rush. It's hard to describe that feeling to the two of you, because you two don't actually do the murders; I do. Neither of you understands how wonderful committing a murder feels. It's different from passion lust, or the pleasurable release of an orgasm. It's more of an excitement thrill. It shoots through the top of my head., like it lifts off the top of my skull. It's a total power sensation. My batteries get instantaneously charged.

'That charge feels like I'm the Devil come to life. And I have all the power in the world, within me. It must be the same way that it feels to be crowned Queen of England. David gives me that same feeling of power and freedom that she has. I'm free to murder my helpless victims; and I'm pleased to have orgy sex with wild abandon afterwards. I love every minute of the experience. And I know I'm safe while committing my murders at David's.

'It's beautiful, erotic, explicit, and horrifying, all at once, Miss Promiscuity. Fireworks go off inside my brain. All my feelings are tightly wrapped in my concentrated emotional surge. I experience

blood lust, life, and death simultaneously. Power over life is entrusted to me! A sensation courses through my blood. I can't explain it better except to say: "If there is divine ecstasy, committing murder is it.

'After I murder, I MUST have sex. I MUST feel a penis in my vagina. The sessions with my murder assistants are the only ones that fully satisfy my nymphomania. Continuing to work with David is MY price. I know David holds that over me; and that, if he gets caught and goes down, then I'll go down, too. That risk is baked into my price. Being beholden to David is MY price. Living with that weird, controlling man in my life is MY price. I love David; but I also hate him. He owns me. I don't like that; but I cannot live without him. I know that. He knows I know that. That's MY price.'

Marty tried to work through her thoughts. She knew she was trapped. She saw no way to escape David's control. Her voices weren't persuasive. She could not quit the murders. Her heart felt a dull, numbing pain, contemplating her future and its implications:

'I especially appreciate you, Miss Iniquity. You have cautioned me about the risks I take by being a murderess. I understand those risks. I know I could be discovered and charged. I'm certain prosecutors would seek the death penalty because I've murdered so often and feel no remorse. But I'm not worried about being caught and charged. I have many millions, thanks to my films and my gifts from Bertie and Gwen. I can hire the best lawyers to get me off.

'Times have changed, Miss Iniquity. Justice in America is only served against people with no money. But I HAVE money. Judges and juries can be easily bought, if you have money. Money prevents a family from getting justice after I've murdered the man of that family. They can't touch me. People with money piss on people who don't have money. That's how it is. David said so. People who believe Justice is blind are fools. Justice is bought and paid for. She's a whore, like me; no better, no more honest, or impartial than me. She does not wear a blindfold. She sees injustice and does nothing.

'Now that I have money, I can't worry about committing murder. If I pay lawyers and jurors and judges, I'll get off. Having my
euphoric feelings of ecstasy; knowing I have the power to play Goddess with a man's life is worth everything. I'll continue to murder
David's problem creeps. I enjoy killing them. At first, it frightened
me. But now I enjoy it. I love watching their blood spurting from
them. I love the empowerment I feel afterwards, while I bond my
soul to theirs.

'It's how I give my love to my father's spirit. I love that power I
feel while I make love in their blood. That tells me that their spirit
understands that my spirit dominates theirs. It's the same as cats
and bears pissing their scents on trees. It's a natural thing for me.
David says I'm doing those men a favor. If I didn't murder them,
they'd rot away in jails. So, Miss Iniquity, don't try to make me feel
guilty about committing murder. I do as I please.'

Marty explained her commitment to murdering while deny-
ing that she didn't understand David. She knew he was dangerous.
But she rationalized her murder partner would never harm her.

'Okay, I understand,' responded Miss Iniquity. I respect your
decision, but please be careful and watch out for David. There's
something wrong with a man who doesn't want to make love with
you after the way you've just put yourself out there for him. I hate
seeing you beg any man to make love with you, especially creepy
David; especially now that you've become a tremendously successful
star of intimate films. Please do less with David and more with your
film career.

'I hear you, Iniquity,' Marty thought to her voice: 'But David
is different from other men. Thanks to Bertie's coaching, I have
empowerment over other men. But David has power over me. He's
not just a pimp with power over his whore. Our relationship is different. He knows me inside and out; where I am; what I'm doing
and with whom; what my money is; how much I'm making on every

gig I'm doing; and he knows what I think. He knows more about me than I know about myself. I suspect that he knows me better than I know myself, but he never mentions that. He holds some overarching secret over my life. I can't put my finger on it. It's as if something is wired into his DNA that somehow communicates with my DNA. Whatever it is, it's real. He knows some secret that gives him a silent power over me.

'I sense that, some day, I will learn where he gets his power over me. Then I will be free of him. Until then, I will do as he says. I will commit murder. David loves watching me commit murder. That pleases him more than anything. I love pleasing him.'

'Marty, please snap out of this! David has you in a trance. Look how good adult films have been to you!' Miss Iniquity persisted. She urged Marty to distance herself from David. *'The whole world idolizes you! Your publicists have brilliantly leveraged your fame up to the stratosphere. Pictures of your vagina adorn millions of magazine pages. Pictures of your smiling face sucking and fucking penises are posted in thousands of men's rooms all over the world. Millions of men masturbate while dreaming they are kissing you and making love with you. They fall asleep imagining their tongues are stroking your clitoris; or that they are hugging you in their beds next to them. You're the woman of their dreams, girl.*

'Your Big Ed's Big Game calendars are already collector items. They sell for over a thousand dollars on the internet. Who imagined that men would pay that kind of money to see your naked poses with hunters and trophy animals? You endorse fifty different products, from perfumes and soaps to clothing lines and automobiles. Your face appears on a thousand billboards advertizing perfumes and lingerie. Your movie downloads earn you millions every year. Famous men, and wealthy men call your service to take you places just to be seen with you. You are in high demand from ultra-wealthy and ultra-powerful men, who want the best and who need to be discreet.

Miss Shameless spoke:

'*She's right. You have arrived, Marty. When people see you in public, they rush to you and scream for you to blow them a kiss or to sign your autograph. You are a world sensation. You've literally become the world's sex symbol. You're about to star in feature-length big screen films. Producers are already making their offers. Their marketing research people estimate that your first film will gross over two billion dollars.*

'*They are willing to contract you to perform in a whole series of big screen films. They've seen your work. They're addicted. They want you to put the same feelings you evoke in adult films into intimate scenes in full length films. If you take half the gross, you could buy a small country and declare yourself Queen. Absolutely, you do not need David. He is a nobody, compared to you. Maybe you believe you need that murder rush, but you don't need that man and his bizarre behaviors! Stop living in the past! Find some substitute for murder. If you must murder, find a new way to do it, without David's involvement. Concentrate on your film career.*

'*Your only remaining competitors are top movie stars of conventional films. And, you are passing those women where it counts: at the box office. All they offer are silly facial expressions, fragile psyches, crazy gesticulations with their hands and bodies, fake love, fake outrage, fake emotions, fake faces, fake bodies, fake everything. Your work is throwing those overpaid nut jobs under the bus; and into the movie history dust bin. The world is moving on from silly clap trap comedy; ridiculous story themes; neurotic producer and director ass kisser want to be actresses; violence; nonsensical movie plots; and men killing themselves from concussions playing football. The world is moving. It's moving to you.*

'*People want to see real love; real emotions; honest, uninhibited lust and sex, presented in reality formats. You've mastered all of it. Many watch your movies ten or twenty times. They study how you move your vagina. They fixate on your expressions while you make love. You've got a deep fan base and you've got fan loyalty.*

'You're a premium box office draw. And you have the reputation of a superior sex mate. When a man wants the world's top sex goddess, he willingly pays your price. Get smart. Make them pay you what you are worth. Make Premium Membership exclusive. Make tens of millions every year.

'If you must commit murders with David, charge him a hundred thousand for each murder instead of fifty thousand. He'll pay. Who else could he get? You're not thinking straight. It's not that the murders only take an hour. It's the money you're saving David! You eliminate his problem people.

'David's business is booming. Each house makes a million a year. He'll soon have fourteen houses. He needs a smooth-running organization. He needs the murders. Don't be afraid of him. He needs you. Tell him you're charging double.'

Marty told her voices to stop their crazy talk. She needed to visit Mrs. O'Dell to hear her shrink's perspective. Much was happening in her life. Her voices were erupting. Her thought processes had become confused and paralyzed. She addressed her voices:

'Before I became a prostitute, I had nothing. Thanks to Mrs. O'Dell and my immorality, I now have everything. I have wealth and freedom to do whatever I please; to take as my lover, whomever I please; to feel no duties to anyone, except David, I suppose; but, with all my freedoms, there's a type of slavery that binds me. I've become a slave of my nymphomania. I'm in a vicious cycle; but I don't want to leave its pleasures. I love it. I'm its willing slave, and David's. I don't know how else to think about it.

CHAPTER FIFTEEN

By the pricking of my thumbs, something wicked this way comes (Shakespeare, Macbeth)

Away and mock the time with fairest show: False face must hide what the false heart doth know (Shakespeare: Macbeth)

BETRAYAL

Marty resumed sharing her thoughts and experiences with David:

"When I leave Bertie's home, Bertie always gives me a dozen freshly baked cookies. She hugs me dearly and tells me to be the best, most beautiful, sexiest woman I can be while working on my films; feel love for my sex partners; and guard against unethical bad people. Bertie always tells me I'm her sweet, innocent little girl.

"I feel a touch of sadness. It's like I'm leaving my own home, where I belong. I hate leaving them. They're so sweet! I never leave Susan's house feeling that way. I love George and Bertie. Never worry that I'd reveal anything about the Firm to them; and I'll never tell them about our murders, David. They're just good people who happen to love intimacy with a sex worker. They're salt of the earth, backbone of America type people, with honest hearts. I just do all the sex things with them that I do with other couples.

"Some couples dress in erotic negligee and sexy briefs. Many like using lubricating oils, soft music, vibrators, and props, like soft crops and feathers. Lots of men and women love it when I queen them."

"Queen them?"

"Oh, sorry. Sit on their face. George loves it. Bertie does too. She gets goofy sometimes. When she's in her playful mood, she sometimes likes to scissors with me."

"Scissors?"

"Sorry, again. It's girl play, David, when we go vagina to vagina."

"We don't peg, squirt, fig or do edging of any kind."

"Peg, squirt, edge?"

"Oh, David, never mind, forget it. I don't do those things for anyone, anyway. I don't care for the excitement of those sorts of things. I don't debase my body or anyone else's. I'm just an old fashion, normal, sex-loving woman. But I love changes of scenery. Bertie and George enjoy sex in different rooms, even in their kitchen and dining areas. It's a psychological thing. It brings out feelings of erotica, every time you go into that room afterwards. They like playing soft bondage games. That's pretty psychological. It can get a little weird, with the boots and whips and masks; but it's harmless and it pleases them."

"I had no idea you did all those things."

"Well, to be appreciated as a good whore to have fun with, I use props and different settings. They create different moods for erotic love making. They also help my client partners' anticipation; and that brings out my own eros. I love the stinging sensation when I'm ass slapped. I love having my heart race from shock and surprise while I'm handcuffed and blindfolded. That's exciting when I'm first penetrated and I don't know which man is inside me, or what he'll do next. What's going on in the mind is the thrill of sex. Stimulation also plays a huge role in having a successful sex practice. Bertie is like many women clients. She loves finger stimulations while a vibrator excites her vagina's crown. I love that, too. Bertie and George both love doing that to me. My clitoris comes alive and goes crazy when they do that. It makes me feel like making love until I'm exhausted.

"*My married couples always ask if I enjoyed having sex with them; if there's anything they could do better; if I'd stay for dinner; or have desert; whether I would consider myself part of their family; all that sort of stuff. Some wives even ask their husbands if their blow jobs are as good as mine. That's when I raise my eyebrows, nod, and blink twice, signaling the husband to answer yes.*

"*Some wives study me while I suck off their husbands. Their husbands think my felatio is heavenly. The wives learn technique from me. I thank Jimmy, my friend and pimp at WEX, for those countless hours we studied porn stars performing felatio. I learned the different techniques for the different phases of the process; how the cock's signals determine what to do and when; and how a woman must love every cock she sucks. Most couples like talking about these techniques. That helps them know me better; get closer to me; and have a more intimate relationship with me.*

"*It doesn't always work out that both the husband and wife want to meet for more sessions. Some husbands call me afterwards and make appointments to see me by themselves; and two wives have called for individual appointments. Perhaps I helped those individuals recognize issues they couldn't face before. And, some other couples' sessions go much better than expected. Some ask if they could bring another married couple that they swap with. I always agree to those requests. I please my customers. Intimacy is a different, limbic mental state, especially when sessions with two couples evolve into orgies.*

"*Mostly, I relish threesomes. They relax everyone's mind and make sex uninhibited, fun, and loving. They are more intimate than orgies. I love them, especially when I'm with a husband and wife.*

"*By the way, David, orgies aren't about hurting marriages. That's a huge misconception. They're not about displacing the wife and redirecting her money to me. They're only about having fun through great sex, getting sales and whatever extra gifts the men give me. It's* true that I use orgies as a way of getting my male partners to love me. They release their feelings to me; place their trust in me. But none of that is an attack on their wives.

"If a wife takes it that way, she's not thinking correctly. Being narrow-minded and unforgiving or vengeful is totally against what Jesus taught. The ones who would punish others for adultery should just forgive and forget. They should be happy that their husbands are releasing their feelings at an orgy with me; and just run along and play Bridge or something. What's girl with an affliction like mine supposed to do, anyway? I'm always after my next conquest. I must have a new lover peel down my panties. Surely God knows that!

"The adultery commandment is a crummy commandment anyway. It's another one of God's mistakes, David. He's not perfect, you know. He makes mistakes, like when he flooded the entire Earth. Really! What was God thinking? Who makes a mess like that? Did it change peoples' behaviors? No. Remember when God had Abraham sleep with Hagar. Look at the problems that caused! That was a disaster! People still fight over which tribe God likes best. What a crazy mess!

"If God didn't want conflict in the world; if God wanted everything to be full of happiness and harmony, God would never have made Sarah wait all those years to have Isaac. But God must want conflicts. That's the only thing that explains it. There's got to be a mean streak in God's personality. God's mean streak must be why we have different religions and different ideas.

"If God ever lets me speak directly to God, one on one, I'm going to advise God to get some serious psychological help from Mrs. O'Dell. By the way, David, God must want there to be sinners too, lots of us; because there are lots of us. And God wants all of us to love one another, regardless of our ideas, our faults, or our sins. So, God, which way is it? Don't sin? Or, sin and be loved anyway? It's terribly confusing.

"David, the way I see it, the wife of a man I'm taking to bed should love me every bit as much as her husband loves me. She should not think her husband and I are sinning. She should be happy for him. She should feel joy, like he feels.

"You know, David, I believe Carl's wife felt genuine love for me. By the way she stared at my cum-filled vagina; by how her lips quivered like they did, I knew she wanted to lick me. But she couldn't admit her love. Her mind was trapped in the ways the world used to be.

"Most people don't have morals. They don't. Movie stars give sexual favors to get acting parts all the time. Housewives cheat. Waitresses, clerks, and secretaries spread their legs for tips and gifts, without even considering the morality of it. Flight attendants fuck pilots; nurses fuck doctors, lawyers fuck their clients; shrinks fuck their patients; and politicians fuck their pages and their constituents. Immorality is America's new normal. That's what's normal. Everyone fucks everyone else. Everyone knows it and nobody cares. Mrs. O'Dell, my favorite shrink, says uninhibited, ubiquitous, iniquitous immorality is the pinnacle of human emotional achievement. She thinks immorality keeps people emotionally healthy in our Modern Morality Standard world.

"David, there's no longer societal stigma over women who make erotic films. It's an honorable career choice. The highest social circles appreciate erotic film art. Adult film stars are congratulated for their latest work. People fawn over the latest innovative films. Coming out parties are given for women to celebrate their first erotic film. New porn stars are celebrated as debutantes. Champaign flows, caviar, and pate foie gras are consumed. New careers are born!

"Intimacy appreciation art is now seen as an expressive personalized art form. It's also an honest profession because everyone knows you're a whore. You freely admit that you fuck for money. Carl's wife simply needed more time to see the world as I do. But she *never gave herself that time. Her mind trapped itself in antiquated thinking.*

"Women in pagan days felt joy when their men went to the temple of Baal and fornicated with temple prostitutes. It was an occasion for family happiness; togetherness, not derision and vengeance. That was before men gained control of the social order. Times were glorious; beautiful. Glorious, beautiful sex is humanity's timeless wonder, David. It's more than a necessity for procreation. That's religion's view. It's more. It's an art form that touches peoples' souls. It transcends and triumphs over moral laws and religious doctrine.

"I don't know why the world left those happy times. I think it happened because men have testosterone. Some men got power crazed. They seized control of the temples, murdered the prostitutes, beat up weaker women and subjugated them. Then they changed the worship rules and invented lots of fairy tales and ordered people to believe the fairy tales. They concocted the preposterous Adam and Eve creation, without conception, story so they could vilify woman as man's temptress and make women responsible for all men's problems. That's how men remade religion. They removed it from its natural beauty and infested it with ridiculous fairy tales.

"Men wrested control of worship hierarchies away from women a long time ago. Worship became male controlled. It subjugated women to males' macho views about how only men should have power. They banned communal love from organized worship; scared the crap out of people with their guilt and hell nonsense; and transformed worship into a chosen us against the outcast them way of thinking. They were usurpers. They screwed up what was once beautiful. But women are making a comeback, David. Paganism is gaining traction everywhere."

David struggled to understand the multiple facets of Marty's mind:

"And what are your pagan beliefs?"

"Simply these: Everything in nature is sacred. I must be responsible for my own beliefs. I believe that women are the central power in the human order of things. I worship all things, with a particular appreciation for the male penis."

"I see. Will you forsake your pagan beliefs when you marry Bob? Will you join a church? Will you stop doing our murders; or will you continue them? And will you still have your affairs and orgies after you're married?"

Marty sought to explain how Bob differed from all her other lovers. *"Bob's a very special man, David." He's the only man that I've ever felt I could love and care about for the rest of my life; so, I have some real mixed feelings about that issue. I don't ever want to hurt him; and once we're married, I would never do anything to hurt him. If he wants to practice organized religion, that's his choice. But I won't go with him to any church. I want him to be totally okay with my immoral beliefs and my film career, too.*

"I think, once he understands that adult films are an art form; and I'm one of the genre's most celebrated actresses, he'll be very enthused about my work. I think every woman, me included, needs one special man in her life. I'm hopeful that after we are married, he'll understand my feelings and just totally love me for who I am.

"Once I'm sure Bob has no inhibitions, and he totally loves me for who I am; once he understands my most intense nympho needs are met through orgies; then I believe he'll want to join me while I'm have those experiences. He already understands that I love making love. By joining me as I release my passions during orgies, I believe he'll appreciate the joy I get from them; and he'll love me even more.

"And, of course I'll continue doing our murders, David. You know how much I love committing the murders. I'll always be your willing partner for that. My nymphomania doesn't preclude me from having a wholesome, loving marriage. Love will over-come any hang ups Bob might have about my nympho disease. I know he'll accommodate my compulsions."

David was more confused than ever. *"You're sure about that?"*

Marty spoke with brimming confidence:

"Yes, David, of course, I'm sure. I'm sure because I know I love Bob and he knows I love him. We feel each other's love. It's solid and unbreakable. Love overcomes everything, David, even my other lovers and my orgies. The only thing that worries me about Bob is his friendship with Barbara. She's very beautiful and she has that slender little girl-like body that drives men crazy. Speaking as a woman, she's enchanting and mysterious. I've noticed how Bob looks at her and how she looks at him. He never mentions his feelings; nor does she. But I see their eyes. For the first time in my life, I know how a woman feels when her relationship is threatened by another woman."

"Ha, you don't need to worry about her. Barbara is very reserved; very prim and proper, and very private. In the years I've observed her, many men have tried to get friendly with her, but none ever succeed. I know you'd like to murder her, but I think you'll discover she's the least of your worries. Besides, we have plenty of time to kill Barbara. She's not going anywhere. There's no rush. If she continues to be an irritant to you, we can always murder her later. We should first groom a replacement for her, don't you think? With things run-ning smoothly for now why should we create a business problem? I understand how much you love murder. But try to be patient. Part of becoming a top executive is recognizing the optimum time to do critical things. We'll murder her when it's the optimal time for the business. Meanwhile, I have a man who is becoming a problem. I'll arrange another murder for you soon enough."

"Oh, thank you for that, David. I'm anxious. Are you just trying to make me feel better?"

"Oh no, not at all," David shook his head in certainty. *"Your marriage journey will have more important things to trouble your beautiful mind and body than that skinny Indian girl. Tell me, though, what about Carl and some of your other lovers? Will they still give us sales after you marry Bob? Can you see them and keep Bob happy? And, what about George and Bertie; will you still see them after you marry? Will you move into their mansion? Will Bob move in with you? Will you have some of your film performers living there, too? Marty, do you even know what you want out of life?"*

Marty's nod was intended to reassure David: *"I've given that a lot of thought. Mostly, I guess, I want my life to have a happy ending. I don't want to be begging on the street or ending up in a flophouse, living on charity. I don't want to be dependent on some man when I get old. I want to have my own family with kids that look up to me, but I don't want to have them yet. I'm not sure what I'd do with them. I never had an example to follow.*

"I didn't have a family growing up. My dog, Barron, ran away. I loved Barron. Then, Dad left me. They say he died in a car accident, but I think he and Mom were just fighting all the time and he wanted to die; so, I don't buy the accident thing. I'm pissed at him. What kind of dad goes away and doesn't come home to his little girl? I needed him! He was all I had!

"Mom was a terrible mother. She abandoned me, took me to WEX school and left me there; just dropped me on my head. So, how in the hell is a five-year-old kid supposed to develop an objective, reasoning mind? Huh? I mean, I am criticized for being reactive to my situations, like my reaction to abandonment was to take up sex and there's something wrong about that. But I don't feel any guilt about my choices. What can anyone expect of a kid who has to grow up without parental love?"

"You really dislike her, don't you? I mean this is something real. You're not pretending, are you?"

"No, David. Not pretending. My feelings for her are dead. They are like a plant that died. I've thrown them in the trash like I would a dead plant."

"But didn't the two of you laugh and hug when you told her you were engaged to Bob?"

"Yes. That was my way of getting back at her. I showed her my engagement ring to make her jealous, because I was getting married and Marvin never offered to marry her."

"But you aren't sure whether you want to marry Bob, are you?"

"No, of course I'm not sure. It's a big decision."

"But you accepted Bob's ring?"

"Yes, of course I did."

"I guess I don't understand women."

"Of course, you don't. You're a man. You're not supposed to understand women. If you were supposed to understand us, you'd be a woman, not a man."

"Some men think they do. They even act like they are women."

"Yeah, but no. Without a vagina a man can't be a woman. They can think they are women; they can wish they were women; but they are delusional, that's all."

"So, I'd need to grow a vagina to understand you?"

"Yeah, David. And our vaginas have mysterious plumbing. You have to grow it in a mother's womb. You're too late to be one of us. Sorry."

"Does Susan understand you?

"Absolutely she does. And that understanding eats her guts out. She wishes she could be me. She was like me, up to a point; but she limited herself. She depended on Marvin and she limited her prostitution to the Firm's pension clients. She wishes she could have had a wide following, like I do. But it wasn't the times for her then. Prostitution wasn't out in the open then, like it is now.

"So, now Mother sits in her office, acting like she has the right to judge me. Huh? Say what? Who does Mother think she is? She has no right to judge me. She failed her motherhood. SO, FUCK HER! She's a shit, David. FUCK HER! She never gave a shit about me. I can't tell you how many times I asked myself why she bothered having me. I can't count that high. FUCK HER!"

"And you don't want to marry; not really, do you? I mean, you're deep down afraid that you'll have a kid and that you'll fail motherhood, too; like Susan failed her motherhood. That's it, isn't it?"

"Maybe. I don't know. I'm just sorting all this out. The only thing I'm sure about right now is that I absolutely, positively love sex. It's an addiction. I know it's an addiction; but it's such a wonderful addiction; and I love my addiction. Can you understand that? David, please. All this emotion is affecting me again. I really need to have sex. Couldn't we have sex, just once? I need intimacy very badly right now. Telling you this stuff about my parents makes me feel extremely close to you, like you really know me. Couldn't we do it together; and become really close, just this once, please?"

David's head eased back. He beheld Marty now as more of a spectre that had not yet assumed its final destined form. He no longer saw Marty as a flesh and blood woman; but as an abstraction in human form that succored the morals of an ally cat. For the first time in the years that he knew her, he appreciated the gravamen of her addiction. It was no less real than a heroin addict's need for a heroin fix. It overrode everything else, even love in all of love's many forms. He perceived, correctly, that he needed to humor her; hold out the promise of giving her that precious sex fix. And he knew that that promise, that hope, was his key to getting Marty to believe anything and to do anything, no matter how implausible or heinous. David now saw that, in Marty, he had everything he wanted and more.

"I feel you, Marty. I really do. We will do it, and soon. But let's finish what we've already started. Tell me your immediate plans. You're going to marry Bob; but what about Carl and the others? And George and Bertie? What are your immediate plans? Tell me. Let's finish this and then I'll make love with you. I promise."

Marty nodded, her eyes were glazed over, as if in a dream. David now understood the depths of her desperation like no one else ever could. Her need for sustenance was not food, not water; but nurturing of a different kind. Her craving was sex. Specifically, it was the male penis and the semen that it flowed to her. It was every bit as strong as a drug addict's need, or an alcoholic's need, but with one major difference. It needed willing partners to satisfy it. It needed the Carl's and the Marshawn's and the Josh's. And the more of those willing supplicants Marty gathered into her orb, the more readily she could satiate her addiction.

He was wary of being sucked in. His agenda traveled a different tangent that he dared not reveal. Not just yet. In time, if and when things fell into place, he would. But if he revealed himself prematurely; if she discovered who he really was, all would be lost. And that could not be! He was David. Chosen. Anointed. Strong. Resolute. She was a woman! Despite his burning passions, he reminded himself that she was his inferior; a woman; not just any woman, but one with unique blood.

Marty resolved to stifle her emotions and finish explaining her plans:

"Okay, David, right now and for the next few years, my immediate goal is to make as many erotic films as I can. I want to build a huge catalogue of exceptional films; including feature length films for the big screen. I LOVE the attention my adult film work gives me. I LOVE knowing men desire me while they watch me having sex. I love walking into a club, having a man recognize me and begging

me for a date. It's an ego thing; having that power to say yes or no to him. My high ranking in intimate film art has put me on a pedestal. It gives me the power to tell my producers how my sex scenes should look.

"I insist that my films are scripted under my direction, with me as the aggressor; or else I won't do them. You'll never see me in a scene where a man insults me, makes me look cheap, hits me, or pushes me down; jumps me; or just bangs me. You see love in every one of my films. Every single time fans see one of my films those fans come away feeling they saw a man and woman deeply in love. They never see some pervert sticking something in a bad place, either. I'm not some animal. I refuse to do scenes that demean me in any way.

"Don't get me wrong. I love doing orgy scenes, but not if the boys think they can shove my body around or get rough. My body is a precious temple and I insist that it be treated with reverence. I like having sex at my own pace. And I insist on respect while I make love. That's it, David. I want to be happy. I need to feel the love while I have sex; I need those giving and taking feelings of endearment. I want to make erotic films as long as I'm on top of that genre. And, when I die, I want my death to have a happy ending. I want to be at peace when I die, that's all. I just hope I never get some long-drawn-out disease."

"And Carl and Josh and Marshawn and your other steady film partners and your steady sales sources, can you tell me what's going to happen with them?"

"Oh, David, don't make this hard for me. You know I love all those guys, especially Carl. Carl is a wonderful, unselfish lover. He licks me wet, and then runs his huge, hard cock along my outer lips until I start to throb and gush inside. I just go out of my mind crazy when Carl first penetrates me; when that huge shaft slips into me. I just can't give Carl up, David, and I won't!

"Whenever I think of him and his hard, monster-sized penis, my panties get damp. I can't wait to wiggle my hips with his huge penis inside me. I come so easily with Carl. He stays hard for me while I come. He makes me feel like my orgasms will never end. No, David, I'll never give Carl up. The man adores me. He loves me; no matter what I do; no matter that I have other lovers. He doesn't have a jealous bone in his body. He lives to give me pleasure and make me happy. I'm confident his sales will be as strong after I'm married as they are now. Every woman should have a man like Carl in her life, even if he isn't her husband.

"And Marshawn, it would be impossible for me to give up Marshawn. Everything Carl is to straight sex; Marshawn is to oral sex. I know I simply can't live without Marshawn. I can't. I won't! I need his intimate intensity; and I need his double-sided, pearl studded tongue. And no loving husband would ever expect his woman to give up the man who gives her so much affirmation and pleasure. I'm confident that Bob will understand and accept my need for sexual satisfaction.

"And Josh, I have to have him sometimes. He plays with my body and makes my blood feel like it's an erupting volcano. Let me put your mind into mine, David. Imagine I'm not a woman. I'm a skyscraper. But I'm an incomplete construction. I dangle magically in mid air. That's how I feel; like I'm up in the air, incomplete. Then, there's Josh, Carl, and Marshawn. They are there to build out the woman in me. They know how to complete me better than any other builders.

"They understand the skyscraper that is a woman's body. But, I'm not an ordinary woman, David. I'm extremely sexual. I'm a nympho. I love sex, but I also want my sexual experiences to be innovative and exciting; never boring. I can lie in bed and have sex, sure. But, why settle for that, when I have expert builders available to me? I welcome the talents of my builders because of their different

skill sets. Marshawn is expert at building my skyscraper from my bottom, up; while Carl and Josh excel at building me from the top down. When my builders complete me, I have spectacular orgasms; like fireworks going off inside me. They are the best lovers; the very best at what they do, David. So, if you needed builders to build a skyscraper for you, would you settle for mediocre workers?"

"No, when you explain it that way, I see your point. I see why you don't want to give them up."

"Good, David. Now you can appreciate my needs as a sensual woman. There are other men I can't give up. You know many of them from our sales reports. I know they'd never give me up either, so yes; we'll still get their sales. They are good lovers. They aspire to become great lovers. I'm working to help them and we make steady progress. I'll keep them as well. I'm relief from their miserable home lives. And they love me.

"And I love those guys back. I love taking four or five of them to a dance club, where all of us can bounce and bump to the fast-hitting drumbeats. I love when the guys unbutton my blouse and unhook me; and unzip my skirt; and then I love feeling them peeling my clothes away from me. I feel like a butterfly, finally getting myself free of my cocoon, fluttering and twirling to the music, swaying with my hands up in the air and running my hands through my hair, while I prance and bump and grind and twerk my vagina, wearing only my half bra and thong; or, sometimes, nothing at all!

"When those guys see my titties and ass bouncing and twerking, they become like wild dogs. They dance close to me. They touch me. They touch their hands to my vagina, my tush, and my boobs. They know that I welcome their touchings. I kiss them and bump against them; and I rub their hands over my tits and vagina. I love watching their imaginations fire up.

"I think about the good, fun time we'll have after we leave the club. I imagine their salty brie cheese-tasty cum spurting onto my

tongue. I'm dreaming while I dance and flutter. I imagine feeling their hot cum spurts gushing over my clit. I imagine their swollen cocks pulsing out bursts of cum deeply inside my vagina. I get myself worked up like that, until I'm positively dying to have sex with them. I'm barely able to contain myself. The men salivate. They want to fuck me crazy after I dance like that. We all love it. It's like we become one unified sexual spirit; like we're reliving ancient pagan rituals. It's beautiful, David. I'm certain we'll still get their sales."

"And you don't use drugs or booze to get yourself hopping crazy for sex like that?"

"Nope, the guys do some of that, but I don't. I don't need it and I don't want to get started on it. It's not good for my body. Oh, I will have a martini after a great romp, a really smooth one, made dirty with three olives. I congratulate myself like that. But that's afterwards. It's more of my celebration of our group experience, and who I am as a woman; but I don't need to get myself sloppy drunk before I have sex; not at all. I relish my opportunities for sex. I don't need drugs or alcohol to make me willing.

"The dance music is all I need. When we're dancing to a live band and I hear the saxophones blaring, the snare drums rapping tat a tat, tat, and the drum sticks hitting the snare rims, while the base drum is pounding the beat; my vagina absolutely comes alive.

"I feel lust fires start stirring inside me. My hot blood pulses to the beat. My clit tendrils heat up my loins. I want to wrap my legs around a man and draw him into me. I know I'm going to have sex soon. My breath and heartbeat quicken. Yeah, I love feeling myself going over this threshold; and becoming this wild fucking machine. I can't wait to start doing it! I get anxious to leave the dance floor. I can't wait for one of my dates to suggest we go someplace quiet. I feel my nymphomania taking hold of me. My voices start talking; telling me to let myself go. Then, I leave my proper self and go into this different world. It happens so fast, David; like in less than a minute.

"I feel this incredible intensity, like I'm superhuman. It comes over me, lightning fast. My skin melts from my heat energy. My body heat gets all charged up, inside me. My soul emerges through my skin. I feel free of all worldly cares. My spirit floats above my body. It watches me dance. I get manic psycho about having sex with my dancing partners. I playfully touch their penises while we dance. I can't help myself. My hands just do that. Suddenly, I'm not the same woman I was an hour before. I'm transformed into this insatiable wild thing; not even a human thing. I'm beautiful, desired, sexy, and free. I glow inside myself. I beam to the men who are with me. My body language screams: 'Come closer. Let me touch your penises. Let me kiss you. Let's go somewhere where you can put your penises inside me; and fuck me. I want to fuck.' Then I press my body against theirs while I dance, touching their penises.

"I'm wild. I'm hot. I'm creamy moist. I'm beautiful, awesome; and I know I absolutely have to have sex. That rhythm and beat gets into my bones; then it stays with me while we're having our orgy afterwards. I bump my vagina hard against their penises while I still hear saxophones blaring in my ears; and drum beats echoing in my brain. I feel like I'm still dancing, while I'm fucking. I'm a wild oversexed animal when I'm excited like this. I have to let my energy out. I can't stop myself. I can't slow it down.

"I can't stop after one or two partners, either. I must do all five of them to release my energy. I'm crazy consumed with lust and fucking. I'm hot and sex crazed; and I absolutely LOVE it! I LOVE doing it while my mind still bounces and bumps in tune with my vagina and the music. All this passion lust keeps flying around in my head. But I do have a small confession, David. When we finish and we're all together; loving, hugging, and jamming I let myself have a drink. I reward myself with a Vodka martini. I like the smoothest, best tasting vodkas. I know the difference. I deserve the best. It fits my goddess mood.

"So, no David, there's no way I'll ever give those guys up. When I'm with them I'm elated. I'm thrilled with being a nympho. It takes time to develop these healthy, meaningful relationships that make me feel that way. Those relationships are honest. I love those guys; and they love me back. They are me. My lovers will all understand my new, married situation. I'm sure I'll be able to work my marriage time in; fit it around my fun times. I'll manage the logistics and make sure all my lovers have their fun times."

"And, you think you'll be able to keep all this straight in your mind and with Bob?"

Marty uncorked a soliloquy:

"I believe so. I've had sessions with Mrs. O' Dell, my shrink, about all these things that are happening in my life; my engagement to Bob; my films; and my choices. She's explained everything. It's all so simple to understand, David. You see, a woman needs more than money, properties, jewels, furs, and things. She also needs emotional satisfaction to be a complete woman.

"She must have emotional satisfaction to become a whole being. She needs penises that love straight sex with her, which are Carl and Josh, in my case. I know they are completely in tune with the wild animal lust that often flares and rages inside me. She needs an understanding, loving tongue for the oral sex she must have to feel she's a divinely worshipped goddess. That's Marshawn. He makes me feel adored and honored like I'm his highly prized, deserving goddess. He gives me beautiful orgasms. I gush uncontrollably.

"She needs to feel omnipotent, outrageously promiscuous, adored and praised as sexy and desirable; and that's why I must make my films; perform in my orgies; and keep my Premium Member Service. She needs to feel she can drive men crazy; and have a man who loves her without having reservations about who she is, or what her needs are. That's my dear, sweet Bob. He gives me that inner feeling of peace, sanctuary, and warmth. His deep well of endless love makes

me feel I belong and I'm accepted without questions or conditions. It's our soul-to-soul love, with our wonderful, tender sex that makes his commitment to me so meaningful.

"You see, David, a well-adjusted woman needs to have all her emotions satisfied, as well as material security. Her emotions complete her. She must experience and express them. She can't possibly satisfy all her emotions with just one partner. That's impossible and unnatural. She must explore, release her sexuality; and find suitable other partners. That's completely normal, according to Mrs. O'Dell. Above all, she must have a healthy and completely satisfied libido; and complete confidence that her sexuality is appreciated and accepted by all her lovers.

"Mrs. O'Dell tells me I'm making terrific progress. I'm the most normal, well-adjusted woman of all her clients. She helps my thinking, immensely. By the way, I explained your theories about how dishonest paper money makes society dishonest and corrupt. She agrees with you, David. She's incorporating your theories into her own.

"She says my nymphomania is symptomatic of society's problems. She thinks stress created by dishonest money has caused peoples' behaviors to become antisocial. People spend less time with their children; care less about others; and have become generally narcissistic. Behavior that was once considered normal, like how I was while Father was home with me, is actually rare now.

"Father died; and then Mother withdrew her love for me to be with Marvin, I turned to sex. Mrs. O' Dell says that stress from Mother's abandonment changed my brain chemistry and made me seek sex as a love substitute. When I finally discovered sex, my brain chemicals rewarded my feelings of promiscuity; and that made me crave even more sex. Sex and nymphomania intertwined and became my normal behavior. Now, the more sex I have, the more sex I want. It's completely normal behavior. Nymphomania is

my self-reinforcing, obsessive-compulsive disorder. But it's normal behavior, because it compensates for my loss of parental love and readjusts my mind so that my mind knows I'm loved. Mrs. O'Dell assures me that the more sex I have, the more normal I am; and the more I'll become like people who had normal childhoods.

"I can't go back to the times before I became sex obsessed, especially now that I'm making adult films. Mrs. O'Dell says I should never try to go back to those times. She tells me I need to continue my promiscuity after I'm married, because my nymphomania requires constant sex; and that's psychologically, perfectly normal, and healthy, given the way my mind works now. She encourages me to continue my adult film career because that keeps me psychologically well balanced and happily grounded in my new reality. Mrs. O'Dell says similar chemical changes, like mine, are occurring in peoples' brains, all over America. More and more, people are behaving more like me! I'm the new normal!

"Children who spend little time with their fathers and mothers watch violent television shows. That's changing their brains to want more violence; so, as those children get older, fighting and killing other people will become their normal psychological state. Their brain chemistry will thrive on committing more violence and more murders. And those behaviors will be perfectly normal for the brains they have.

"In Mrs. O' Dell's opinion, every passing year more women will turn to nymphomania, and more people will turn to violence until we get rid of the Federal Reserve Bank of the United States and go back to honest money. She believes we'll eventually do that. Then society will gradually become peaceful and family oriented again.

"She believes our entire society has been a gigantic abnormal laboratory experiment, using dishonest money for our experimental sample population, versus the honest money we previously had for our control sample, before the Federal Reserve's bankers invaded our society; and versus the honest gold and silver money that some

other countries use. She thinks our ill-fated experiment with dishonest money has run amuck and failed; and it will end. She thinks if it doesn't end in a planned way, society will collapse in a disorganized way. Then, we would lose empathy for our fellow man. We will become numb to murder and rape. Crime will become a normal happening and common part of everyday life. We'll become immoral creatures, like many insects.

"She thinks my work in intimate films will save the world from destruction. She's excited about my upcoming series of erotic films for the big screens. She confided to me, David, that on a personal level she loves watching my girl with girl oral and scissor sex films. She told me they get her all hot and creamy; and when I come, I make her drool. I can tell she's developing a love interest in me.

"I love Mrs. O' Dell. She understands me, like George and Bertie do. She wants me to get married to Bob because she believes Bob connects me to my childhood normalcy and family love. She says I must also continue doing films and my Premium Member Service. If I ever stop, my new Modern Moral Standard brain chemistry will get out of balance, and I could become an emotionally unstable person. It's also important that I experience new lovers on a regular basis. I'm well-adjusted now. And I must continually strive to do more of what pleases me, to stay well-adjusted.

"I agree with her. I almost go crazy when I don't know if or when I'm going to have sex again. I only feel secure when I know I'll have sex again, soon. That's why marriage will be perfect. I can make love with Bob every single night before I sleep, or whenever I awake in the middle of the night with my night sweats and my insatiable fuck craving. Now, when I apply Mrs. O'Dell's theories to our murders, the murders make perfect sense to me.

"The more people I kill, the more I look forward to killing the next time. I just can't help it. I love the feeling I get from murdering, especially the nirvana feeling I get afterwards when you reward me

by letting me have my orgy. I think the murders have changed my brain chemistry, too. That must be true because I can't wait to do them. I'm anxiously looking forward to our next one, David. I promise you; my next murder performance will be the most sensational you've ever seen. You're going to love watching me."

"I see. What about George and Bertie? Will they be okay with you getting married?"

"George and Bertie will accept anything I decide. Of course, I'll continue seeing them. Our love for each other is very real. They are like parents to me now. I've mentally adopted them as the loving parents that I lost as a child, and the bonus is that I make love with them, and get paid for doing it. I totally love them! After Bob and I are married I'll discuss with Bob the idea of moving into their west wing. It might work out great. That wing is three times larger than my house and Bob's house combined; and, who knows, maybe George and Bertie will want to have foursomes with me and Bob; and maybe Bob and I will be invited to join them for their swap parties. I know many people would think a lifestyle like mine, where there's so much sex and so few boundaries, is not workable and crazy.

"But, you see, it is workable and it's not crazy when people understand that brain chemistries and hormonal responses are changing society because of our dishonest money. More and more, people are going to think it's perfectly acceptable and normal to be having affairs and swapping partners. Mrs. O' Dell says it's the natural reaction response of people under stress to connect with others and have loving relationships with them; in many cases outside their marriages; and no one should feel any shame or guilt about it."

"Good, Marty. Bertie and George sound like a lovely couple. Maybe they'd love watching you commit murder as much as I do. We'll have to do another one soon. By the way, did I ever explain to you what a loose end is?"

"No, you didn't."

"*Well, tell me what you think it means.*"

"*I only know what it means for some of the girls who do porn. They say it's a vagina that's open for a penis, and a mouth that's ready to give head to a penis. It means ready for action.*"

"*Well, it can also have a different meaning. In business it means a problem or a risk that needs to be tied up, or ended.*"

"*Okay, what are you getting at?*"

"*You told our secret about doing murders to Bertie and George.*"

"*Yeah, so...? It was an honest slip-up. I told Bertie I wasn't thinking straight because of a headache. I covered it. Besides, Bertie said she'd never tell anyone.*"

"*Marty, there's something about people you need to understand. People can't keep secrets. None of them can. Everyone who hears a secret must tell it to someone else. That makes them feel accepted, trusted; important to the other person. It's a human need thing. No human can keep a secret, no matter how many safeguards you put in place. It is not possible to keep a secret, secret. It's an incontrovertible truth. Bertie and George are loose ends now.*"

"*What are you saying, David?*"

"*I'm saying they know something they shouldn't know. That gives them power over you. That's not smart. Tell me, how much do you need them?*"

"*I love them. They are like parents to me.*"

"*That's not the question I asked you. How much you need them? Don't you already know everything you need to know to make outstanding films? Haven't you got the best directors, hairdressers, beauticians, manicurists, make-up artists, and porn partners now? Aren't they already contracted to your production company and locked down?*"

"*Yes.*"

"*Okay, you also talked on and on about how Bertie taught you so many things. How much more can she and George possibly teach you? Aren't you already the number one ranked star of worldwide porn? Aren't your films getting downloaded at five times the rate of the next five girls combined? So, what more do you need to learn? So, again I ask you, how much do you NEED them?"*

"I guess I don't actually need them to make my films better, when you put it that way."

"Good. Now, pay attention. You need to understand what it takes to be a top executive, to be number one. Think for a moment about Hitler, Stalin, and Mao. Whenever they thought someone was close to sharing their power with them, they simply murdered them. They were ruthless."

"Yes, I've learned about them."

"Good. Your goal is you've decided to become the world's number one star of erotic film; and one of the top executives at the Firm, right?

"Yes, absolutely, those are my goals."

"Okay, then think what could happen if word got out that this Bertie and George couple helped your techniques to make you number one."

"I don't understand, David. What?"

"Marty, Marty, put your mind into their minds. Once word gets out what they can do to make an actress number one, there will be twenty other women seeking their help to become number one. They could displace you, take your position away from you. You see, to George and Bertie you are just a toy to have sex with; and you are helping them advance their own importance. You can't take the chance that they will not someday turn against your interests. You need to think like Joseph Stalin would think."

"What are you saying, David?"

"I'm saying you need to totally lose your morality if you truly want to be number one. You can't be a fool. You can't live your life by the Ten Commandments or the law. You can't believe in established

institutions like the silly U S Constitution or its stupid Bill of Rights, either. You can't believe there is a god. You can't think you must honor a father and mother. You must be willing to lie, cheat, steal and murder. You can't have a conscience about doing whatever it takes to give yourself power over others. You can't let anyone or any established order get in your way. To have power you must take power. So, why would you take the chance that Bertie and George could use their skills to displace you from being the world's top erotic film star?"

"I guess that would be foolish of me, wouldn't it?"

"Yes, that would be terribly foolish. That would give them power over you. Now, can you see that they are a risk to you? They also know something they shouldn't know. That gives them the ability to take your position away from you. That makes them a loose end."

"Yes, I see what you're saying, David."

"Good. Then we need to tie off this loose end."

"What are you telling me, David?"

"I'm telling you that you would honor me greatly and I'd appreciate your honor if you'd help me get rid of them. I want to help you achieve your goal. I want you to stand alone as the world's top intimate actress, the world's most sensational porn star. I don't want anyone else to have the ability to take your glory away from you. I'll make sure they can never do that to you."

"How, David?"

"I want you to help yourself by arranging their murders. Don't feel any guilt, Marty. They should have known better than to put themselves into a position to take away your glory. They should have known better than to take you into their trust like they did. They did that to have power over you; and to find out things they shouldn't know. Now they have become......"

"Loose ends," Marty caught on. She finished David's sentence; smiled, and giggled at him. The devilish idea of betraying her friends and murdering them suddenly titillated her, even though

Bertie and George were like parents to her. Suddenly, she discovered the ability to stab those who love and trust her in their backs. She began thinking like a communist.

"Then you'll do it?" David believed Marty's thrill of committing murder trumped all her other desires. He sought reassurance that Marty had no moral compass.

"Yes, David, for you, for me, for us; and with you, of COURSE I'll do it. Murdering my dearest friends will be so wicked, so completely immoral!" She squealed at the prospect of the future thrill.

"Yes, I'll love stabbing Bertie. How dare her try to take away my power? We've outsmarted her, David. This will be a fabulous murder, my best ever! I'll spill her guts out, then listen to her cry and scream. I'll stab her while George watches; and then I'll murder George. The shock on their faces will be priceless. Would that honor you, David? Would you like to watch me doing that? Would you love me and make love with me after I take care of our loose ends?" She embraced David tightly, hinting at the pleasures she would give him. The idea of secretly committing two more murders with David flooded out Marty's conscious thoughts.

"Very much so." David squeezed her back. *"It would almost make me feel like you and I shared our same blood, so to speak. After you kill them, only the two of us will know what evil pleasures we have. No one else will know our secret, right?"*

"Yes, David, that's right. Only the two of us and our two assistants will know then. Can we celebrate by making love then?"

"Yes, I promise you we will; but not on that same day. I want it to be just the two of us and on a very special day, okay?"

"Yes, David, of course, anything you say."

"Good, Marty. Then I want you to invite them to my farm. Tell them there's a wine cellar they simply must see. Lure them into the guillotine room. I'll take it from there. When they awake, they'll be

tied up. You can shock them by saying your good-byes. Then, you will plunge your knife into them. You can enjoy hearing their cries and screams. You'll thrill at the horrified looks on their faces. I'll be honored to watch your performance. It will be an immoral event I'll always savor."

"Yes, David, we'll have a wonderful time. It will be my honor. I love you for all you do for me, David."

"I love you, too, Marty. Now, may I ask about your marriage arrangements? Will Bob be okay with you having other intimate partners and making adult films with them? How do you think he'll feel knowing you've been having an orgy on set all afternoon; and then, you're home with him, just the two of you? Do you think he'll want to have intimate relations with you after you've done seven other men?"

"Oh, yes, I really believe he will. In my own loving, caring way, I believe my extramarital liaisons will make me more sensuous with Bob. I desperately want him to be a happy husband. I'm sure he'll love me more, knowing that I'm a happy, well adjusted, free woman. He knows my film art is a huge part of my freedom. He knows it's important that I discover new partners and new lovers. I'll just make everything work, David. I won't pretend that I don't make erotica. Making love on set gives me such a wonderful rush, David. Making those films; having sex with new partners is addictive. I love it. Bob already knows that about me. He knows I won't stop making adult films just to marry him.

"I love feeling the lights, the cameras and all that attention focused on me. It's my self- empowerment, David. It's something I'm proud about. I don't need to depend on a man to keep me. I earn more in one year making my films than most men make in their lifetimes. My erotic art will be my wedding gift to Bob. It will be my way of telling him that I'm with him because I love him; not because

I need him to support me. And I do love him, David. I love him dearly. When I'm with him, no one else matters. We laugh and love and play together. We love each other's company.

"And, so what if I'm a prostitute? Who cares? No man wants a deadpan wife who doesn't enjoy making love. Men don't think much of women who are afraid of living life; who just sit around sucking their thumbs. A man prefers a woman who loves sucking his penis; and if she loves sucking other men too, well, that's so much the better. Bob will see things my way. He'll get it. He'll be glad to have a total woman who expresses herself freely; and who fucks and gushes openly, and often. Loving and being loved is freedom's ultimate expression."

"This Mrs. O'Dell shrink really helps you, doesn't she?"

"Oh, yes, David. She helps me understand everything. Mrs. O'Dell's main theory is that there are two different standards of societal behavior. There's the revolutionary new Modern Morality Standard, which is followed by progressively minded people who live in the present and look forward; and there's the Cultural Standard which is followed by regressive-minded people who live their lives looking backwards. Behaviors of people who live by the Modern Morality Standard sometimes clash with behaviors of people who live by the Cultural Standard, according to Mrs. O'Dell.

"Mrs. O'Dell says that many people still follow the morality of the Victorian era's Cultural Standard. That standard held that a woman should be a virgin until she married. The woman's virtuousness and submissiveness were praised, and seen to be a desirable feminine behavior. Her husband broke her hymen on her wedding night. That was her symbolic opening to her husband. He owned her after that. Her duty was to service him sexually, as well as to cook for him; clean his house and bear his children.

"For the husband, the wedding night was analogous to a little boy ripping away the wrapping paper of his birthday present. More

people living today are choosing to live by the Modern Morality Standard. They dismiss the Victorian Cultural Standard. They see society has progressed and that modern women's needs are greater than the needs of Victorian era women.

"Many of today's women still need a husband to provide for their income needs, but their needs do not stop there. They also need romantic fulfillment and stimulating erotic experiences. Those needs mandate that women have multiple lovers and sex partners, in addition to their husbands. This is perfectly understandable and normal. It's healthy for a woman to have confidence knowing that many men love her and love having sex with her. That builds her self esteem. That's a good thing and there's absolutely nothing wrong with that.

"There is no stigma or dishonor for today's Modern Morality Standard women to freely engage in extra marital relationships or have frequent and long-lived sexual liaisons with many different men. In fact, women who openly practice this Modern Morality Standard are sought out by many men, as wives or sexual partners. These women make ideal wives. They are highly prized by today's males.

"Mrs. O'Dell says this is due to declining male sperm counts. She thinks the sperm count needed to be high when men had to hunt down and kill meat for the family table in Victorian times. It was a virile, manly thing to kill game to provide for the woman. Nowadays, men go to the grocery store to buy meat. They don't need to be manly to kill for meat anymore. They can cross dress and play women's sports. Their maleness is disappearing. That's why their sperm count is declining.

"Today's men are much like women. This enables their thoughts and feelings about women's needs to be more sympathetic with modern women's New Morality Standard behaviors. That is why the males' concept of what constitutes a desirable woman to marry has

changed so radically since the Victorian era. Back then, a virgin was highly desired for a marriage partner.

"Nowadays, adult film stars and women with erotic performance experiences are highly prized and sought after by men seeking marriage. Today's male wants his wife to be sexually and emotionally liberated, free of inhibitions; and, preferably, highly experienced in every type of sexual expression and love making; including participation in orgies and enjoyment of BDSM. If his wife is notorious for her performances of explicit sex acts on screen, she automatically becomes a premium, highly desirable marriage partner. The world is rapidly adapting to the Modern Morality Standard. Men, and many women, are falling head over heels in love with their prostitutes.

"Since Victorian times moral standards have come full circle. We've returned to temple prostitution worship, just like in pre-biblical times. Whores are no longer despised; they are revered. Marrying a prostitute is now a male's ultimate passport to high social status. An adult film star wife is like a lustrous diamond, enhancing her husband's image as a liberated man who embraces the New Modern Morality Standard.

"Receiving an invitation to an adult film star's wedding is confirmation that you have arrived in the highest social circle. Weddings to erotica stars are widely publicized and heralded as must-attend social events that often include orgies as part of the celebration's festivities. Having a celebrated adult film star wife gives a man access to social functions and networking opportunities that barred him previously. Husbands of adult film stars are seen as open-minded Modern Moral Standard practitioners who champion their wives' promiscuous proclivities. The modern liberated husband fully endorses her dalliances and extra-marital affairs.

"Today's progressive, Modern Morality Standard male expects and supports his wife; and does whatever satisfies her emotional

and sexual needs. He wants her completely free to pursue self indul-gence and sexual satisfaction. A good male partner encourages her participation in intimate film art performances; and he actively promotes her work. He is the non-possessive complement to her life. After Mrs. O'Dell explained these things to me, I know I'll be very happily married to Bob.

"You'd love Mrs. O'Dell, David. She's a real businesswoman. She has a dating service that complements her shrink practice. She pairs up men and women who seek Modern Morality Standard partners. So far, she has about ten men for every woman enrolled in her ser-vice. She advocates that all her women patients should join her dat-ing service; and make at least three adult films with new partners to unleash their emotions; and fulfill their suppressed needs from living the outdated Cultural Standard. She says the Modern Moral-ity Standard is eclipsing the old standard at a fast pace."

"She's out to change the world, isn't she?" David nodded his approval.

"Yes, in many ways, David. She's a revolutionary Avant Garde thinker. For example, she thinks people who turn to violence are just unfortunate because they haven't yet learned how to cope with the Modern Morality Standard. They try to force the old cultural stan-dard upon those of us who have moved on. These men beat unfaith-ful wives and the women kill their husbands who cheat on them; and so on. Mrs. O'Dell thinks these people are victims of rapidly changing morals, dictated by the new Modern Morality Standard. They haven't acclimated. As a result, they get frustrated and go crazy.

"She believes more women should enter erotic film making, or at least discover the benefits of having multiple sex partners; and she wants many more women to join her dating service to acceler-ate social change. She also thinks violent criminals would be cured of violence if a tax-payer funded, government program would pay

them income and dating money so they could form loving, long-term relationships with prostitutes. She's certain that would reconfigure their brains and turn them into productive, non-violent lovers."

"She thinks the government should pay for violent criminals to have sex? That seems crazy!"

"Yes, she does. Why not? She has a good point. I've never heard a prostitute talking about bombing some other country or making more missiles, ships, and planes so we can kill more people. Whores don't think like that. They think about making love. Mrs. O' Dell thinks society has its priorities completely backwards; and women need to rein in the men. She wants the whole society to turn away from violence; and turn toward love, sex, and honest money. She says it's time to try something different because what we're doing isn't working.

"She thinks everyone should have steady loving relationships with prostitutes. Whores should be welcomed into peoples' homes and accepted as family members. They could provide valuable sexual variety to the husband and wife. They could help with child rearing. They could explain the Modern Morality Standard to the children.

"She wants careers in prostitution to be widely encouraged, like George and Bertie encourage me; and she thinks prostitution should be offered as career, major study courses in schools and colleges. Why not? Whores are joyful and fun loving. They spice things up and make stress much more bearable. Mrs. O' Dell thinks everyone should make the effort to get to know several prostitutes and adult film stars; and include them in their circle of close friends.

"I love Mrs. O'Dell. She's a great, clear-headed thinker, and she's so sweet! She wants to compartmentalize our relationship into the professional and the personal. She will continue being my shrink on our appointment days, but on our free days we will simply be best friends and explore our girl-girl emotional and sexual needs

together. We're having our first girl's date tomorrow night. She has hinted that we'll share vagina kiss-kiss sex."

"What makes you think so?"

"Well, I can tell she wants to do it."

"How can you tell?"

"Well, during our sessions she fingers herself while I describe how I feel during my orgasms with men. She says stimulation helps her understand my feelings. So, I think she'll want understand my feelings when I'm with her, too."

"And you're okay with your shrink behaving this way?

"Oh, yes absolutely! I can't wait! I want us to kiss each other everywhere. She said she'll help me become completely liberated and totally in tune with the new Modern Morality Standard."

CHAPTER SIXTEEN

Mad, bad, and dangerous to know. (Lady Caroline Lamb: Her Journal, of Byron)

There are two kinds of love. There's love, love. That's chocolates, roses, dinners out, socials, and travels. Then, there's insane love. That love fires your blood passion, claws at your guts, and shreds your soul from the inside out. It's the one you'll do anything to get. (Rosemary Ness-Bitner, author)

INSANITY

"That's beautiful, Marty," encored an enthusiastic David. *"I love how your mind works. Your mind is beautiful. Everything about you is free and beautiful, like your glorious vagina and your lovely butterfly tattoo. Thank you for helping me understand everything perfectly."* as David spoke, he decided it was pointless to try to think about things in the same ways Marty did. He kept his thoughts to himself:

'There are so many things I love about Marty. She doesn't have hang ups about morality like most women do. She took a sledgehammer to her moral gyroscope years ago. She's perfect for the Firm. She steals, cheats, lies, seduces, murders when I tell her to, and loves doing it; and she never questions my instructions. She seduced Bob at my direction and kept him in the Firm, away from Barbara.

'She's captured the loyalties of at least twenty salesmen through her whoring and that brings in a steady stream of sales; and she's

landed some big sales of her own. She likes to destroy marriages and send idiot women to the poor house. I love how Marty destroys their lives. Most women are useless, pretentious, nitwits anyway. I like it that Marty doesn't put up with them.

'I love knowing she has no loyalty to Bob, even though he's, her fiancé. She's recently engaged, yet here she lies, naked with her legs spread wide on my hay bales, begging me to fuck her. She's the perfect, model employee. I must admit to myself that I do love her. I've loved her since I first saw her when she was a little girl.

'But there's been a change. She tried to conceal her engagement to Bob from me. She disobeyed my instructions about romantic involvement. She wasn't supposed to go that far. She was only supposed to seduce him and charm him, add him to her stable of lovers; not fall in love with him. I know from experience that if someone will lie about even the smallest thing, they will also lie about anything and everything. So, this is not a good situation anymore.

'Now there's this Bertie business. Marty thinks this woman is her new substitute mother. She's intimate with her and her husband. And, she's breached our secret to them. She's gotten out of control. She says she is about to become intimate with her shrink, too. They're going to play "Vagina, Vagina, Kiss-Kiss!" How sweet! Am I supposed to be okay with that?' David shook his head in disgust.

'Who knows what will happen with these cunts getting intimate with each other? They're women! Women can't keep their mouths shut. They always have to emote. They have to "feel." They have to puke and blather-spew their feelings all over each other; and get hysterical about the stupidest, most inconsequential, banal things. How long will it be until Marty lets her shrink know about my murder chamber and my body disposal operation?

'I'm right about her,' David's thoughts tormented him. *'She wants to be married to Bob and have her lovers and her orgies and*

her film career, and her intimate girl friends. And she wants to emote all over the place like a leaky bucket. She wants it all. She wants to have her cake and eat it too.

'This decision is hard because I love her. I know I love her. She overcomes my preference for men, somehow. It must be my attraction to her wantonness. Our minds are so much alike. I do so much deeply love her. She lies there, believing that sex will change things between us. I don't know. Maybe it would. She has no idea how much I love her. She's family to me. She loves evil and sin as much as I do; maybe even more than I do.

'I suppose I should make love with her. I desperately want to, but it would be wrong to defile her. I must NOT defile her. That wouldn't read well in the Book of Life. I don't want to piss off my rabbi. He knows me too well. He knows everything. But she's so purely evil and sinful; and she's completely innocent and beautiful and pleasing in her murderous lewdness.

'I know I shouldn't make love with her. I'd be taking away her innocence, her purity. I'd be crossing that forbidden barrier. I know it would be beautiful. I can already imagine it. Yes, it would be unforgettable. How could I ever explain such an impure deed to my rabbi? He might ask questions. He might find out about the murders. I can't risk it.

'Should I tell her I dream about her; about mounting her; even getting rid of my wife and marrying her? She could control me then. But when she knew our truth, she could tell my rabbi. One word from her would ban me.

'This is the fault of her Goyim mother's blood! Why couldn't Father have fallen in love with a Jewess? Damn you, Father! You've left me with this mess! It's complicated. I need to think. So horrible! So unthinkable! She's very tempting. She wants to make love with me. She's sincere all right. I also want to make love with her. It's hard to resist her. It's practically impossible.

'If only she were pure! I can't lie. I couldn't pretend I didn't know she wasn't pure. There's the red streak. That blemish doesn't lie. I'm losing my mind here. I know I am. I can't think straight. Maybe I should surrender to her and let come what may? I don't know what to do. I must do the right thing and the smart thing. Which is it?

'Adonai, help me. I love her. I want her so much. It's our blood! Our blood cries out. Our blood wants to join together. Her blood calls to mine, begging to join. I can't stand by and let her beg like this. It's not our way! What am I doing? I need to decide. But I must make the right decision.

'Maybe if I talk to Dolly about this, everything will make sense. My mind is spinning out of control. Oh, Marty, I love you. I love you. I love you. Adonai knows how much I love you. He knows I dream of you. He knows I want you. He knows I don't want to ever give you up. You are my most precious possession. You are the best any man could ever possess! I want to take you into my arms and hold you close to me forever.

'Wait! I just had a thought. Yes. I had a beautiful thought. I CAN hold you. AND I can love you! AFTERWARDS!'

CHAPTER SEVENTEEN

*The thirst to know and understand, a large and liberal discontent;
these are the goods in life's rich hand, the things that are more excellent (Sir William Watson: Things that are More Excellent)*

*Learn; pass your test and rest. Awaken then, and flutter west
(Rosemary Ness-Bitner)*

KALEIDOSCOPE

Butterfly Poon was exhausted. Her mind twirled from all the things
she'd heard. She needed essential rest before her kaleidoscope fluttered away on the morning sun. As she fell into her slumber, she
wished she knew more about humans.

*'What were they like as little humans? Were their lives as inter-
esting as caterpillar and butterfly lives? What was the man Bob like,
the one whom Marty was obsessed to possess? Were they as obsessed
with their romances and their mating as Monarchs? Did they have
the same behaviors that their parents did, like we Monarchs? Did
they obsess about how to get where they are going, without ever having been there before, like us butterflies?*

*'And who,' she wondered, 'is the mysterious Barbara woman,
whom Marty thinks is Bob's true love? Was Barbara some kind of
super sex-goddess? Marty seemed to think Barbara was a natural
leader, but she didn't talk much about that. How does one human
lead other humans by remaining quiet and staying in the back-
ground, like the Barbara woman does?*

Marty's world intrigued little Poon. But now Poon was falling asleep. She prayed that the Great Spirit of All Living Things would permit her spirit to join with the spirits of these human people so she could understand their emotions. What compelled them to do the things they did, like commit murder? She prayed to the Great Spirit to show her their lives from their beginnings.

'What were Bob and David like as little boys? How did they come to know each other; and what events transpired to place Marty on those hay bales below? Did all human women display their sexual anatomy that way? We butterflies only do that once; briefly, in mid-air, before we mate.

'Why did Marty speak openly of her insatiable lust for other men and her deeply devoted love for Bob? I only have love feelings for Tang. What must it be like to have love feelings for so many males? And what compels Marty to desire David, when she already has Bob? Why does Marty work for David? Who made David? Did he have parents? Why were these two humans here together in this barn? Why is Marty envious of Barbara?'

Poon wondered more about the mysterious Barbara, the beautiful, silent woman who knew more than all the others. *'Did she also love Bob?'* And Poon wondered about Carl's wife. *'Why did she drive off that mountaintop? Would other tragedies intersect the lives of these humans?'*

Innocent Poon wished she could fathom what it was like to think like a human and be like one of them. Many more developments would unfold after Poon fluttered off to the wilds of Chiapas, Mexico for her glorious rendezvous with Tang. She hoped her next generation's spirit soul would also rendezvous with these humans.

Before she slept, Poon prayed to the Great Spirit:

'Please, Spirit, let my journey be safe and please, Spirit, somehow, let me become a human woman like the beautiful, voluptuous

Marty who knows no limitations to her promiscuity. Let me feel Tang, that huge male Monarch between my legs. Please let me meet Barbara so I can discover why Marty feels threatened by her. Help my spirit bond with the lives of these fascinating humans. Help me understand their lives, as they have lived them.'

A deep slumber came over Poon. She was a third generation Monarch; one that had to migrate south, to be reincarnated into her fourth life. Her spirit would return from her migration in her offspring, to meet with humans again; and her offspring would repeat her spirit's cycle of life. She said a big prayer to the Spirit to hear her:

'Oh, great U, Spirit of all living things, please hear me, a tiny butterfly fluttering as best she can in your vast, wondrous, hard to understand, world. Please let me meet with Tang again and mate with him above the Mexican jungle canopy.'

When morning's sunlight warmed her, Poon awakened and bravely fluttered onward. She left the humans behind and joined her kaleidoscope of Monarchs, believing her prayers would be answered; comforted in knowing that her progeny would flutter back this way for years to come. Her spirit would live inside them and they would also meet these humans. Her spirit would discover that the humans also feel passions and needs; and they would discover, as she did, that every human, like every butterfly, is special.

More to come.

PREVIEWS OF MOTHER'S LOVERS

"There's nothing we can do to stop David's evil spirit from doing what it will do. You know evil is very powerful; but we can curse the human in which the evil spirit resides, so that the human will die and the evil inside that human will lose its host. We butterflies are not without our ways, you know. We are not to be trifled with . . . . .Chapter One.

The rabbi had raised his index finger to the side of his eye and emphasized the demarcation between man and God. *"God hears the fatherless child who cries out to him! God is the one who hears the afflictions of the fatherless! Torah says God upholds them and brings them justice. There is nothing in the Torah that says this is your duty, Arlene. Only in the Tanakh is justice mentioned for the fatherless."* . . . . Chapter Two.

After the game and safely at home. Arlene asked her husband Morris why the crowd got so out of hand.

"It's because they want revenge," he answered knowingly.

"Revenge? Revenge for what?" She didn't understand the Teutonic psyche as well as Morris did.

"Revenge for being who they are, I guess." . . . . . .Chapter Two.

"He keeps digging in the dirt because he wants to find his father down there in the ground. He said they put his father into the ground; and he's going to find him and get him out of there."
....Chapter Three.

"You came 'ere to learn how to deal with kids, so you listen carefully to old Alma. I don't let kids have no feelins. Feelins is like horseshit. They's soft, mushy, and useless. I'm 'sponsible for dere 'bedience and dere learnin, whiles they 'ere. Dat's 'nuff! When one of 'em starts up with feelins, it's the whip for dat little bastard
....Chapter Four.

"Ashes to ashes, dust to dust. From the Earth we came and to the Earth we return. Into *thy hands, Almighty God, we commend our brethren's spirit* .... Chapter Five.

'If separation was the true reason for the mechitza, why then,' Mendel reasoned, *'did not the men and women alternate Shabbot services, taking turns behind the curtain? Why was it that men always had to be the closest to the Holy of Holies and the women always had to be seated the furthest away* .... Chapter Six.

'Should you decide to marry and have children with another man, that will be your business. Neither I, nor you, shall ever speak of our relationship to your husband, or to your child, or to my wife, Eloweiss ....Chapter Seven.

"Would you like to have me, Joseph?" She asked while French kissing him.

"Yes, oh God, yes," he moaned.

"And you won't feel guilty about being with me instead of Bonny?" Susan teased while kissing and licking the head of his penis ....Chapter Eight.

'*Poor bastard,*' thought the sheriff. '*He's working his ass off out on the Western slope, away from her, while she's probably busy in the city, fucking some other guy. The poor stiff probably loved her while she was heartlessly clawing his guts out.* . . . . Chapter Nine.

"*Mavin, did you notice? He was also wearing a wedding ring.*"

"*Doesn't matter. Actually, makes a liaison with you that much more appealing. I trust what his eyes were telling me. He wants you.*"

"*I know he does. I'm a woman. I can tell when a man wants me.*"

"*Well, then?*" . . . . Chapter Ten.

Dear listeners, that concludes BUTTERFLY TRADECRAFT the sixth segment of our series. Little butterfly Poon has heard Marty explain why all women will become more promiscuous with time. And, she's learned that the personalities of David, Bob and Marty were all shaped by unusual childhoods. Now she wonders how Barbara, a child from a closely knit family, will interact with the others. Barbara is beautiful, mysterious, and driven to succeed, but why is she this way?

Can demure Barbara control her romantic urges as her father commands? Will she gain Bob's trust and his love, or will promiscuous Marty crush the two erstwhile lovers' budding romance? And, what profoundly dark evil secret is David concealing? Will Marty actually murder her best friends to please David? Did our characters' formative years create adults with characters every bit as fascinating as a Monarch's metamorphosis?

Be very aware of David, dear listeners. He's tormented by indecision and he's up to something. He's the evil one. And evil never rests. What's inside his devious mind? What might force him to reveal himself? I'm Melanie Monarch. Let's learn more about these unusual humans. Flutter along with me as I voice MOTHER'S LOVERS, the seventh installment of THE SECRET BUTTERFLY (tm) SERIES.